What people ar

It had been a gruelling day...

Dylan returned to the castle early evening. It had been a gruelling day, after being up all night and then having to discuss his designs at a meeting with a local firm. He set his brief case down in his office and went in search of Stephanie. He had been a little hard on her, he knew that. The gentlemanly thing to have done would have been to explain the situation beforehand about his so-called engagement to Cassandra and also that she was employed as his new manager. But instead, he had known how to hit below the belt by using shock tactics.

He knocked on Stephanie's bedroom door, but there was no reply. Cassandra came up behind him carrying a pile of towels.

"Are you looking for Steph?" He nodded. "She checked out a couple of hours ago. She said to thank you for picking her up safely from the airport and for giving her a room for the night."

He opened his mouth to say something and closed it again. Stephanie couldn't have winded him more if she had punched him in the gut. He couldn't believe it. Why on earth had she left when she knew that her life was in danger? He found his voice. "Do you know where she went?"

Cassandra shook her head. "I know she was asking for the phone numbers of local hotels but each one she tried was booked up as it's the Christmas season. I think she mentioned something about going back to her apartment to pick up her things."

"Cass, I need to find her..." He didn't wait to hear her response. Stephanie's life might be in danger and it was all his fault.

TO

Karen

Return To Winter

by

Lynette Rees

Best wishes

Love from

Lynette Rees x

Return To Winter

Contact Information: info@thewildrosepress.com

Cover Art by *Tamra Westberry*

The Wild Rose Press
PO Box 706
Adams Basin, NY 14410-0706
Visit us at www.thewildrosepress.com

Publishing History
First Crimson Rose Edition, April 2007
Print ISBN 1-60154-061-2

Published in the United States of America

Dedication

To Mrs. Robinson,

The teacher who encouraged me with my writing when I was fourteen years old, you regularly read my stories to the class, allowing me to believe I could tell a good tale.

Chapter One

Stephanie's stomach fluttered. Her mouth dry, she tried to settle back into her seat and relax. Relax? How could she do that with her heart in her mouth as she trembled from top to toe? She hoped the passenger sitting next to her wouldn't notice her discomfort. She wished now she'd taken a gin and tonic from the trolley earlier, to take the edge off her nerves.

"Fasten your seat belts..." The pilot's voice interrupted Stephanie's thoughts. The plane was about to land at Heathrow airport—she was finally home. Nine months was long enough for anybody to be on the run.

Glancing across at the stranger sitting next to her, she smiled nervously. The elderly lady offered her a stick of chewing gum. "I always chew gum when we take off or land, helps with the pressure in the ears." Stephanie leant over and accepted a stick. The last thing she wanted was an earache when she met Matt and Sandy at the airport.

What would they think of her? Leaving their wedding reception in a mad dash? She hadn't even had time to say goodbye to them. And Dylan...she dreaded to think what must have been going through his mind only moments after they made love. How could she explain the real reason for her swift departure? It wasn't going to be easy.

The plane prepared for descent and the elderly lady reached out for Stephanie's hand, giving it a reassuring squeeze. "It's hard when you're a nervous passenger." She smiled. Stephanie nodded, it was better to let her think that than the real reason for her anxiety.

****

Dylan parked the car and walked towards the airport

1

terminus. She would have some explaining to do when he saw her. His mind wandered back to that early spring afternoon at the wedding. It had been a wonderful day, not a cloud in the sky. It had all gone off without a hitch; the only cloud had been her departure. One moment he was touching her silky hair and kissing her soft neck, inhaling her musky perfume, and falling asleep basking in the afterglow of their lovemaking. The next he had turned over in bed to see the imprint of her head on the pillow. All that was left of her was the scent of a woman and a couple of strands of dark auburn hair.

He swallowed. This wasn't going to be easy. How was he going to feel coming face to face with her again? More importantly, perhaps, how was she going to feel coming face to face with him?

If Sandy hadn't been rushed to the hospital, he wondered if he would have known that Steph was back in the country at all. No doubt she would have asked Matt and Sandy to keep it a secret from him. He blew on his gloveless hands. It was freezing. The weathermen had predicted snow. Snow at Christmas time? Didn't happen that often in Britain, did it? There were only four days left to the big day itself. He hadn't given it much thought other than in a work capacity. There had been the Christmas fashion show he had put on a fortnight back for the Cancer Concern Charity, but other than that and getting his grandmother a present, there was no Christmas spirit for him. Bah Humbug!

He put his hand in his pocket and pulled out a silk scarf. He'd found it in the corridor shortly after Stephanie performed her 'Cinderella' act. He held it to his face, inhaling her intoxicating perfume again. The smell was a powerful trigger for his emotions; it brought back the moment when he'd held her in his arms for that sensuous first kiss.

****

Stephanie lifted her suitcase from the luggage carousel and headed towards the 'Nothing to Declare' sign. Was this all she had to show for the past nine months? Milan had been wonderful; she'd stayed with her grandparents at their tiny apartment, finding work at a local family-run hotel as a receptionist. She could have stayed longer, but something was missing from her life. *Something or someone*, a little voice reminded her.

Thankfully, she would have time to catch her breath beforehand and prepare what she would say to Dylan. Matt and Sandy could fill her in on the details of how he had reacted when she'd left, and what he was doing now.

Castell Mynydd, the castle he had bought with his father, had been a good investment for his fashion business. He had branched out into Celtic bridal wear, intending to offer the full package of providing the outfits, reception and honeymoon at the castle. By all accounts, by the time Matt and Sandy had their wedding there, he was fully booked for the following year.

It wasn't just running out on him as a lover that made her feel bad. He had also offered her a job at the castle as a manager and she'd let him down, badly.

She hesitated as she walked through the arrivals area and searched the sea of faces for Matt and Sandy. Maybe they had been delayed? The announcement of another plane due to land startled her, so she felt slightly disorientated. The background noise became muffled to her ears as striding towards her in the throng, she spied a familiar figure.

She stopped, unable to gather her thoughts. Her breaths came in short bursts. *Dylan*. Something was different about him. What was it? His blond hair was a little shorter than she last remembered it, but it suited him that way. He'd put on a little weight too. She'd thought he was a little too thin before, now he appeared more muscular, filling his jacket quite well

For a moment, her mouth felt dry and her legs turned to jelly. She took a steadying breath. "Dylan..." she said, unable to say any more.

"Save it, Steph," he said, tearing her suitcase from her hand and casting a thunderous look that made her want to dissolve into the floor. "The car's over here."

She followed after him like a puppy dog. He didn't look at all pleased to see her. She didn't get it. Why was he picking her up and not Matt and Sandy?

When they stepped into the ice-cold air, she found her voice and called out after him, "Hang on a moment, what's going on?"

He stopped, put her suitcase down and turned around to face her head on. "Look, I've come to pick you up. You want to get back to Wales sometime before Christmas, don't you?" She nodded. "Then get in the car."

She did as she was told. He put her case in the boot and slammed it shut. He was blazing angry. She'd never seen him in a temper before. Mild mannered Dylan Pryce-Jones was seething. This was going to be difficult, him not talking all the way home. She let out a long breath, closed her eyes and pretended to sleep on the long journey back to Pontcae.

****

Dylan glanced at the woman sitting next to him with her eyes closed. It was hard being so close. How could she expect him to be nice? Perhaps he should have explained the situation, why Matt and Sandy hadn't been at the airport for her, yet why should he? She had run out on him without a word of explanation. He hadn't even found out which country she had been in, until today. No, he'd let her stew a little longer. He intended to hurt her just like she had hurt him. It was hard not knowing where someone was, especially when they chose not to tell you.

The silence got to him and after a while, he switched on the radio.

"For all you Christmas lovers out there...here's a golden oldie..." the D.J.'s melodic voice cut in and faded away to the tune of 'White Christmas'. He switched it off. White Christmas? There was no sign of it so far.

"Hey, I was listening to that!" Steph sat up in the passenger seat.

"Tough. Anyway, I thought you were asleep?"

"Just resting my eyes—that's all."

He looked across at her. It was hard to remain angry with someone as beautiful as Steph for long.

"So are you going to tell me why you're here to pick me up and not Matt and Sandy?" she asked, pausing for a moment as if about to say something else.

"Not unless you tell me why you ran out on me at their wedding..." He gripped the steering wheel, starting to feel the red mist engulf him again. "I'll stop at the next service station, then we can talk." That would be much safer than trying to drive while getting wound up.

"Err..no. Leave it. I want to get home as soon as I can."

He knew she was lying. She probably didn't want to talk about things. "Well I'm the driver; I'll decide when I want a rest, if that's okay with you?"

"Yes, of course it is. But we'll leave the conversation for some other time."

He said nothing but carried on driving, switching the radio back on.

Twenty minutes later, he pulled into a service station and parked. "Coming?" he asked, getting out of the car. She shook her head. "Suit yourself."

He needed to get a cup of coffee to stay awake. It was three in the morning; he had a meeting first thing. Damn the woman. He was putting himself out for her and she wasn't even grateful. Not only that, but she didn't seem to think she owed him an explanation.

As he crossed the car park about to enter the brightly lit building, he heard footsteps behind him. "Dylan, wait for me." He carried on walking. "Hang on...I'm sorry. We'll talk." He turned to face her. She frowned. Was she worried about something?

"Come on then," he said, softening a little, "let me buy you a coffee."

She smiled, but somehow it didn't quite reach her eyes. What had been so bad that she'd had to leave the country at such sort notice? He was about to find out.

****

Stephanie watched Dylan standing by the counter paying the waitress. Was she dreaming? Was she really here with him? Any minute now, the alarm clock would go off, she was sure of it. The smell of fresh pastries and coffee wafting over, told her this was no dream. As he turned around to bring the tray over to the table, she glanced away; she didn't want him to know she had been studying him.

"I've bought some sandwiches, too," he said, setting down the tray.

"Thanks."

"BLT, okay with you?"

"Fine." She emptied a sachet of brown sugar into her coffee.

"So, are you going to tell me what happened?"

"Tell me where Matt and Sandy are first."

"Sandy's been rushed into hospital. Which reminds me, I need to ring to find out if they're okay…"

"They?"

"Oh sorry, you wouldn't have known would you…she's having a baby."

Stephanie spluttered, almost choking on her coffee. They were fast workers; it must have been a honeymoon baby. They hadn't mentioned it when she'd phoned them to pick her up.

"I know what you're thinking…but she's not due until the beginning of January. It looks as if the baby's decided to put in an early appearance." He grinned then his face clouded over. "So come on then…what happened?"

She hesitated for a moment. "I don't know if I should tell you…"

"Damn it." He made her jump as he banged his fist on the table. A middle-aged couple at the next booth looked at them and he lowered his voice. "Sorry, but you owe me that at least, Steph."

"The reason I don't want to tell you is because I was, still am, in danger, and I'm afraid if you get involved you might be too."

He looked at her incredulously and started to laugh. She felt hurt. Didn't he believe her? He gazed into her eyes, searching them as if to discover if she were telling him the truth. The laughter ceased. "You're serious, aren't you?" Leaning across the table, he took her hand. "Look, you need to tell someone if you're in danger, the police…"

She retracted her hand. "No police…definitely not the police. If I tell you, you must swear not to tell anyone else unless I say so."

He nodded. "You have my word."

"When we were at the wedding, someone turned up. Someone I didn't want to see."

"But I don't understand. You were with me most of the time."

"After we made love…" She felt her face grow hot as she struggled to say the words.

"So what—that's hardly a crime…"

Pushing the embarrassment away, she continued.

"You fell asleep and I dressed and went into the reception area for a bottle of wine. I saw someone there, I'd rather have not seen."

"Who?"

"Perhaps I'd better not tell you." She chewed on her bottom lip.

"For goodness sake, Steph—this is getting like riddle me ree!"

She took a deep breath. "Lawrence Black."

"Matt's friend? The one who loaned him his apartment while he was overseas?" She nodded. "I don't get it."

"Before he left, he promised he'd come after me. He's into all sorts, Dylan. Importing heroin, organized crime..."

"Really?" Dylan lifted a brow, then looking more serious, said, "What's he got on you, Steph?"

"He murdered someone." She shivered momentarily, swallowing a lump in her throat and could hold back the tears no longer.

"But how do you know that?" he asked gently.

She turned away, brushing a hand against her face. She didn't want to cry in front of him. "Because I saw him do it..."

****

Dawn was breaking by the time they arrived in Pontcae. The only vehicle around was the milk float.

"You can't go back to your apartment at the Bay, Steph. You'll have to stay at the castle until something is sorted out," Dylan said gravely. He didn't know what to think. Could she have somehow been mistaken? She nodded. "We'll talk later. I have an early meeting, so there's no bed for me. You can have a good sleep; you must be exhausted after your trip. You'll be safe here with me." He hoped that would provide her with some comfort at least, but in his heart of hearts, he wondered just how safe she was from a man like Lawrence Black.

Something he had to do when he got inside was to ring Matt to find out the news about Sandy and the baby. After the shock announcement from Steph, it had totally gone out of his mind. So she hadn't run out on him purposely. That was good news. But was her life in danger? That was the question. How could he protect her?

She wouldn't let him contact the police. And what about Matt? He was a friend of Lawrence's. Could he shine any light on the matter?

****

As they pulled into the castle grounds, Stephanie's stomach lurched. She hadn't been here since running off from Dylan at Matt and Sandy's wedding reception. The castle looked somehow eerie but beautiful in the half light of dawn. She had only seen it in daylight before. Its turrets and arched windows now prominent as spotlights emphasized their shape and structure. A young blonde woman came out to greet them wearing a red silk kimono and bedroom slippers. Even at this time of the morning, she looked amazing. Not a hair out of place, it seemed she'd just left a beauty salon rather than a bedroom.

"Who's that?" Stephanie asked, trying not to sound too interested. She felt taken aback that there would be another woman at the castle.

"Oh..." Dylan hesitated, "that's Cassandra..."

"Cassanadra?"

"Yes, she's my manager."

Stephanie felt as though her heart had been pierced by an arrow. She bit her lip as she fought to hold on to her composure. No way did she intend for either of them to see her reaction. That was the position she had been about to take if she hadn't gone off like that. Dylan was hardly to blame though was he? He'd had to fill the void she'd left behind. Seeing Cassandra only served to remind her of how badly she'd let him down.

As she got near to the car, Cassandra's face broke out into a broad smile.

Dylan opened the car door and stepped out, the woman ran into his arms. "It's great to have you back, darling," she said breathlessly.

Darling? This didn't sound like the greeting you gave your employer.

"Steph, meet Cassandra, my fiancée."

For a moment, it was as if time stood still. She couldn't believe her ears. He couldn't have missed her that much when she ran off to Italy if he had got engaged to someone else so quickly. The ground appeared to rise up towards her as her sight blurred with unshed tears.

"Pleased to meet you," Cassandra said in an artificially refined accent. The woman sounded common as muck. She was trying to sound posh, but making a hash of it.

"Likewise," was all Stephanie managed to say in reply—the lump in her throat was in the way, and she was totally bereft of any friendly feelings towards the woman. Any chance she thought of her and Dylan getting together was now thwarted.

"I'll have Cassandra show you to your room," Dylan said, not appearing to notice her reaction to his news. "I'm off to shower before my meeting. If you want some breakfast, it's being served to guests in the dining room in half an hour."

She thanked him and watched him head off in the opposite direction with not so much as an "I'll see you later..."

She followed meekly behind Cassandra and a porter who carried her suitcase. Cassandra was wittering on about her and Dylan, but Steph wasn't taking it in. Damn. She had missed her chance. Damn Lawrence, damn Cassandra and damn Dylan.

When she finally got into her room, she lay on the bed, shuddering with emotion. Tears welled up and spilled down her cheeks, her heart was broken. The only man she had ever loved was due to marry someone else.

****

Dylan took a cold shower—he needed one after being in Stephanie's company. What was it about the woman? She did something to him that no other woman ever had. The effect she had on him was astounding. When he'd touched her hand in the motorway services on the way home, he'd felt a shot of electricity. His nerve endings still tingled thinking about it. His thoughts turned back to the afternoon of the wedding. When the speeches were over, she'd asked to explore the castle with him. She'd taken no persuading when he'd dragged her into a vacant bedroom. They'd collapsed together on the bed and made love to the strains of Burt Bacharach on the radio.

He had been convinced that this was the woman he wanted to spend the rest of his life with. What he'd omitted to tell her was that he was already engaged to someone else, but at the time it hadn't seemed to matter. He would have called off his engagement for her, but she hadn't given him a chance. Instead she'd run away from him.

Cassandra had been his childhood sweetheart. They'd been an item at school for as long as he could remember. Yet, when they became engaged, they'd spent a lot of time apart from one another: university, then his training in Hong Kong, and she had worked in a bar in Spain. So they hadn't really had that much of a relationship to speak of. Yet, neither had got around to breaking off the engagement. So it had been a perfect opportunity when he was told Steph was arriving from Italy to introduce Cassandra as 'his fiancée'.

He knew in his heart that he and Cassandra wouldn't be together much longer. She preferred to stay in London and he loved Wales. Two separate people who no longer had school in common. Cassandra knew it was over too...it was only a question of time.

He was jolted back to the present by the sound of his mobile ringing. It was Matt.

"Any news?" Dylan asked.

"No, not yet. Sandy's resting. The doctor says if she rests up she may go full term."

"You mean the baby may be born in January as it should be?"

"Yes. She may be allowed home tomorrow. Did you pick Steph up okay?"

"Yes. She's staying at the castle." He toyed with sounding Matt out about Lawrence, but then thought better of it. He didn't want to step on Steph's toes. She'd sounded upset enough as it was and her face was a picture when he introduced her to Cassandra.

****

Steph yawned and reached out for her watch off the bedside table. It was almost midday, she'd missed breakfast, but at least she could have some lunch. The reality of the situation hit her again and she felt a gnawing pain in the pit of her stomach; this was nothing to do with hunger, not hunger for food any way. This was down to the searing pain she felt at losing the only man she had ever loved.

From the day she had first met him at Sandy's dinner party, they had got on like a house on fire. They were friends to begin with, but the wedding reception had changed all that. That afternoon they had crossed the line from friends to lovers. Could they ever go back again? Could she be satisfied with just friendship from him? The one thing she did know was that she needed him in her life, even if it was just as a friend. The only cloud on the horizon was Cassandra. Would she allow her fiancé to be friends with a woman he had once been intimate with? She very much doubted it.

She ran a shower and wondered what to wear for lunch. How did one dress for meals at a castle? There were several guests staying at the hotel with it being the Christmas season. Eventually she opted for a smart black pair of trousers and a red lamb's wool sweater. At least she would look festive.

The dining room brought back memories of that last afternoon with Dylan. It had been in here that the wedding reception had been held. The wedding had been quite a small affair; the banquet room was used for larger weddings. At least the dining room made her feel less anonymous; she would have been totally lost in the other room.

When she entered, a waiter smiled at her and asked for her room number. The oak-panelled walls gave the room a medieval feel, but strangely enough, it was decorated in a Victorian style. A large real pine Christmas tree stood in the corner, adorned with lighted candles. The staff were dressed up in Victorian period costume and a string quartet played in the corner of the room. At the far end, a log fire blazed in the huge, stone fire place.

Whatever anyone said about Dylan, he went about things in a big way, paying attention to detail. As she seated herself at a table she spied a familiar face entering the room—Cassandra. She carried a clipboard and spoke to someone wearing a white chef's hat and apron. She could have been doing Cassandra's job herself right now if she had played her cards right. It hurt to see someone else in her place.

Cassandra caught sight of her and strolled over, looking the picture of efficiency.

"Ah, Stephanie. Nice to see you again. How long will you be spending with us?"

The thought was left hanging in the air as one of the guests cornered her. That was a very good question indeed. How long would she be spending at the castle? She just didn't know. If things had worked out differently, then maybe she could have said, indefinitely. But with Dylan's fiancée on the scene, perhaps she would be better off making alternate arrangements.

A waiter came to take her order. The menu reflected the Victorian theme and Steph opted for roast duck and all the trimmings, a half bottle of wine and a sponge pudding for dessert. After lunch, she rang around some hotels. She was afraid to go back to her apartment until she was sure that the coast was clear. That was the problem, she lived in the opposite block to Lawrence. She could practically see into the living room of the man who wanted her dead. She couldn't even go to the police...if Lawrence found out, she'd end up six feet under.

****

Dylan returned to the castle early evening. It had been a gruelling day, after being up all night and then having to discuss his designs at a meeting with a local firm. He set his brief case down in his office and went in search of Stephanie. He had been a little hard on her, he knew that. The gentlemanly thing to have done would have been to explain the situation beforehand about his so-called engagement to Cassandra and also that she was employed as his new manager. But instead, he had known how to hit below the belt by using shock tactics.

He knocked on Stephanie's bedroom door, but there was no reply. Cassandra came up behind him carrying a pile of towels.

"Are you looking for Steph?" He nodded. "She checked out a couple of hours ago. She said to thank you for picking her up safely from the airport and for giving her a room for the night."

He opened his mouth to say something and closed it again. Stephanie couldn't have winded him more if she had punched him in the gut. He couldn't believe it. Why on earth had she left when she knew that her life was in danger? He found his voice. "Do you know where she went?"

Cassandra shook her head. "I know she was asking for the phone numbers of local hotels but each one she tried was booked up as it's the Christmas season. I think she mentioned something about going back to her apartment to pick up her things."

"Cass, I need to find her..." He didn't wait to hear her response. Stephanie's life might be in danger and it was all his fault.

Chapter Two

It was biting cold as Stephanie got out of the taxi and paid the driver. She would normally have given him a generous tip, but all her small change was in Italian currency. She turned up the collar on her jacket, not at all prepared for the British weather. Glancing across at Lawrence's apartment, she held her breath, then let it out again. All appeared to be in darkness. With any luck he might be away, visiting family in London or even out of the country. His cyber cafe and two nightclubs in Cardiff and Newport kept him busy.

She found her key, tapped in a security code and let herself into the well-lit building. Immediately, she switched on the lights. Lawrence could be there waiting for her right now. But how could he possibly know she would turn up at this very moment? He had probably been as baffled as Dylan had been about her sudden disappearance. The apartment felt icy cold and smelled a little musty. After all, it had been without an occupant for the past nine months; she had managed to keep up the payments by Visa card from Italy.

Putting down her suitcase she scooped up a stack of mail, bills and junk mail mostly, intending to go through them later. Then she went into the kitchen. The cupboards were bare except for a few tins and a stale packet of sponge fingers, the only thing she had forgotten to throw out when she had got rid of all perishable goods before leaving the country. There were still a few things in the freezer. She filled the electric kettle and put it on to boil. At least she could have a cup of black instant coffee. There was some frozen bread, she could have a couple of pieces of toast and there was an unopened jar of marmalade on the counter. She'd have to do without the butter for time being. If she was holed up here over Christmas, she could at least have some food to keep her going. There were a few other things in the freezer she could make good use of.

If she was careful, and kept the place in darkness, Lawrence need never know she was here at all, and then when she got herself fixed up with a hotel, she could leave.

She whirled as a voice came over the intercom. Holding her breath, she thought for a moment it might be Lawrence. "Steph, let me in…" This was not Lawrence's husky smoker's voice. Mildly irritated, she realised it was Dylan. What did he want? She ignored it.

"Steph, are you going to leave me here all night? I know you're in there."

Sighing, she pressed a button to allow him access. "Come up," she requested.

As he entered the apartment, a look of concern swept over his face. "Are you okay?"

"Yes…" She hesitated. For a moment, she thought she might cry.

He put his hands on her shoulders and looked directly into her eyes. "Why did you leave so suddenly, again? You have a habit of doing that."

His grey-green eyes darkened as he spoke and she wanted to melt in his arms, for him to kiss her one more time…

"I…I thought it was for the best," she managed to reply.

"Best? Best for whom?" He furrowed his brow.

"For you and Cassandra."

"Well it certainly wouldn't be best for me, I can assure you."

Why was he saying this to her? It sounded as if he really wanted her in his life. Perhaps he was just a typical bloke, wanting his cake and eating it, to have two women on the go at the same time? Exactly like her father had been with that mistress of his. She'd never forgiven him for abandoning her and her mother. Can a seven year old really understand why a parent leaves?

"You're not going to need me around if you have her, are you?" She gritted her teeth and clenched her fists into

15

balls at her side.

"Of course I need you. You mean so much to me. When you were away..." He didn't finish his sentence. What had he been about to tell her? His eyes were fixed on something behind her.

"What's the matter?" Something was wrong. She could see it reflected in his eyes.

"The mirror behind you..." was all he managed to say.

She turned around quickly. Scrawled on the mirror in lipstick were the words, "YOU'RE DEAD!"

Nausea rose to her throat and she took in a sharp breath. How hadn't she noticed it before? But she hadn't really looked around the room, had she? She'd dropped her suitcase and gone straight out to the kitchen to make coffee.

"He's been here, Dylan. Lawrence has broken into my apartment. He wants me dead!" The room spun and her vision blurred.

"Steph, are you okay?" She heard Dylan's voice, but couldn't focus...then the room faded to black.

*****

Stephanie felt like liquid in his arms as he carried her over to the sofa and laid her gently down. If anything should happen to her...

"Steph," he tapped her on the cheek. "Steph..." Her eyes flickered open and she looked at him through a haze of unshed tears. "Are you all right?" She nodded. He caressed her cheek with the back of his hand.

"I'm sorry. I guess I haven't eaten much...then the jet lag." She sat up and looked at him wide eyed. "Dylan, I don't know what to do. If I stay in Pontcae my life will be in danger."

"Are you sure Black's not one of those people who shoots his mouth off?"

"You don't know what he's capable of. Remember I saw him murder someone."

"Yes, but you don't know that for sure do you?"

"Believe me, I know what I saw. I can see into his living room window, my apartment overlooks his. He had his hands around a woman's throat, throttling her. I didn't know what to do. Moments earlier they had appeared to be having some sort of a row, and then she smacked him across the face. He grabbed hold of her arm and kissed her passionately."

"There we are then, a lover's tiff."

"You don't believe me do you? You think it's my over active imagination. I know what I saw. Besides, a couple of days later the local paper printed an article about a woman who had gone missing. The article said it was out of character for her not to have told anyone her whereabouts. The photograph in the paper was a bit faint but I felt I had seen her somewhere before."

"Sorry. I can understand your concerns." He lowered his gaze. "Go on."

"As I watched Lawrence with the woman in his apartment, they appeared to make up. Then, as they were kissing, his hands moved to her neck, stroking it tenderly. Then his grasp got tighter and tighter. I could see the woman's eyes getting wide with horror."

Dylan looked directly at her. "Come on now, Steph; how the hell could you see all this in so much detail unless you had a pair of binoculars?"

She smiled. "I have a telescope. I've been watching his comings and goings for months. He has a courier turning up regularly on a motorbike who he hands a parcel to."

"So what, he has a business doesn't he?"

"Yes, but his business is supplying people with drugs, mainly heroin."

Matt blinked in disbelief. He could easily believe that Lawrence was a small time crook, but one of the big boys? It would cost him a fortune to import heroin.

"He has the perfect opportunity with his business concerns," she continued.

"But how do you know all this?"

Her face clouded over, "I used to work for him..."

For a moment he stood there, unable to take it all in. How could someone like Steph get involved in the drug scene? When he came to think about it, what did he know about her at all? Only what she had wanted him to know.

"How long ago was this?"

"A couple of years back." She bit her lip.

"What kind of a job did you do for him?"

"Anything and everything he wanted me to. You see Dylan, it might sound as if I have no scruples, but one thing you have to understand is that he was blackmailing me."

"Why?"

"Lawrence Black is a very manipulative person. I'd go as far to say he's a psychopath."

Dylan held up his hands in despair. "So how did you get involved with a person like him?"

"I worked at one of his night clubs in Cardiff. He showed a lot of interest in me. It was flattering at first. I mean, you know my background. Abandoned by my father as a child, so an older man paying me that sort of attention was intoxicating to say the least. Well, anyhow, I can see now that he was grooming me."

"Grooming you?"

"Allowing me to think what a nice, kind person he was, so that he could get me to do anything he wanted." Suddenly, she looked weary. "He bought me lovely things and made me feel special as if he was always looking after my interests. Then he made out that he was interested in me in a romantic sort of way. He made me fall for him. I thought I was in love at the time as I had nothing to compare it with, but now I've experienced the real thing, I know it was infatuation with him."

Was she talking about their love affair before she went away? Or had she been in love with someone else? "Go on…" He urged.

"The next step was promoting me at work so that I became a hostess, responsible for taking care of clients at the club, business men and scum balls. Anyhow, I soon realised that being a 'hostess' meant becoming a 'hooker', so I left the club. He came after me and persuaded me that he'd never force me to do that and he loved me and wanted to marry me. I fell for it hook, line and sinker. I went back to the club and while I wasn't a 'hostess' like some of the other girls, I knew what was going on, I'm ashamed to say. You see, he videoed a lot of the action and used the tapes to blackmail people." She paused. "Some of the men were threatened by his heavies that if they didn't cough up, a video would be sent to their wives. It wasn't just their sexual antics on the tapes, but drug taking too; snorting coke was a regular occurrence at the club."

"But if all of that went against your moral code, why didn't you just leave him?"

"Because he'd asked me to do a job for him involving Matt. When Matt first came back to this country after working overseas, Lawrence gave him the keys to the flat; this was when he and Sandy first met one another. He sent me over to seduce him and plant drugs on him."

Dylan couldn't believe his ears. This was a side to Stephanie he had never seen before. A darker side that he didn't much care for. How on earth had he got involved with her? By rights he should walk away. "So you set Matt up for him?"

"No. Not exactly. You see, I couldn't do it. Matt wouldn't sleep with me anyway, but we did become friends. And of course, he met Sandy and I was really sorry after I tried to mess things up for them."

"But if you didn't really do anything, then what has this man got on you?"

"I made the mistake of telling him that I'd seen him strangling that woman."

Dylan didn't know what to think. He didn't doubt for one second that she was telling him the truth. But to be involved in such a seedy world as that, it didn't bear thinking about. He could tell she was upset as she relayed the story to him, he'd noticed her bottom lip trembled as she spoke.

****

"So what do we do now?" Dylan asked gently, putting his arm around her.

She noticed that he said 'we' and not 'you', that was comforting to hear.

"I just don't know, Dylan. I could clear out of here for good, there's nothing to keep me here anymore…"

"How about me? And Matt and Sandy too?"

"You're part of a couple now, Dylan. You don't need me around to mess things up for you."

He raked his hand through his hair. "You don't understand, Steph. All is not as it seems. I should have explained properly. Cassandra and I are on the verge of splitting up; our relationship is going nowhere."

"I don't understand, Dylan. Then why did you get engaged to the woman?"

"We've been together since school days. Got engaged a few years back, but through circumstances of us being parted so frequently, we hardly got to see one another."

She felt the heat rising as she exploded. "So what you're really telling me is that when you and I slept together at the reception, you were already engaged?"

He nodded. "I'm afraid so. But I swear it isn't an engagement in the conventional sense."

Hot tears welled up inside her. How could he have done such a thing to her and his fiancée too?

"Get out of here! You disgust me. You and men like you. Leave me alone."

He went to put his arm around her again, but she recoiled from his touch. "I can't leave you here, Steph. It's too dangerous. Just pick up some of your things and come back to the castle with me. Stay over the Christmas period and see if you can find somewhere after the New Year."

"Dylan, I don't intend to spend one more night than I have to under the same roof as you!"

She turned around and looked directly into his eyes. Love and compassion shone in their depths. "Steph, what other choice do you have? What kind of a man would I be, leaving you here as prey for someone as evil as Lawrence Black?"

All was silent for a few moments, then she spoke, "Okay. But only because I have to. I want you to keep as far away from me as possible."

He nodded. If things didn't work out, she could always spend a night or two at Matt and Sandy's, they had a spare bedroom. She wouldn't bother them unless it was absolutely necessary with the new baby on the way.

Dylan reached out for her hand. "Friends?"

"I'm still thinking about it. I wish I could hate you, but I can't. Just promise me that you'll keep away from me if I come back to the castle with you?"

He smiled. "It will be difficult, but I'll try my best. Now pick up your things and let's get out of here before Lawrence gets back and notices a light on."

She rummaged in her wardrobe and picked up some

sweaters, jeans, a pair of boots and a padded jacket to take back to the castle, along with her suitcase. She'd need those the way the weather was turning.

****

Dylan sat in an armchair in the drawing room of the castle. It was late. Midnight. He hadn't slept in over twenty four hours. The adrenaline had kept him going; there had been bucketsful of that to contend with. First, finding out that Stephanie was back in the country, then, having to pick her up from the airport and finally, discovering she was on the run from a dangerous man, and on top of all that, Sandy's difficult pregnancy. Why did life have to be so complicated?

He considered ringing his father to ask his advice about Lawrence Black, but decided against it. He didn't want to drag him into the situation as well. It had only been little more than a year ago that he had found out who his father was. The papers had had a field day with that one, "Famous Fashion Designer Fathered Illegitimately!" He'd known that his mother had been pregnant at age sixteen to a much older, married man, what he didn't know was that the man would turn out to be the Right Honourable Conservative member of Parliament, Sir Reginald Greenaway.

After the initial shock, he had been united with his father, who despite appearances was delighted to meet his son. His mother had been mortified. To all intents and purposes, Dylan was her mother's child; he had been brought up more as a brother than a son. So there were severe consequences for her, he supposed. She was the only person who was against him meeting up with his father. He wondered why? Which is why he intended to reunite them at the castle at Christmas. His mother would be arriving on Christmas Eve, his father on Christmas morning. Neither knew about the other one's arrival. Sparks were sure to fly. Maybe it would be the wrong time for this reunion with what was going on with Stephanie, but wheels were in motion and the air needed to be cleared.

His mother had got divorced only a couple of years back and his father became a widower last year. He'd never gone on to have any more children, which was probably why he was delighted to discover that he had an heir. Yes, Christmas was going to be an exciting time with the friction between his parents and himself and Stephanie. Very exciting indeed.

Chapter Three

Whatever Stephanie thought about Dylan, she knew he had her best interests at heart, even if he did have a closet fiancée. She wondered if they were sleeping in the same room right now. She only had his word for it that they were living separate lives. Men often lied about that sort of thing. Yet, he'd never been dishonest with her before had he?

She undressed, put on her night gown and picked up her hairbrush from the dressing table, studying herself in the mirror as she gave her hair its usual one hundred strokes a night. There were a couple of dark circles under her eyes, nothing a good night's rest wouldn't cure.

Tomorrow was Christmas Eve. She had been invited to spend time with her mother on a trip to Scotland over the festive season, but had politely declined at the time as she'd intended staying abroad when she was asked. Now she wished she'd accepted. Family was something she needed right now. Family, and to be far away from Pontcae, Dylan and Lawrence Black. If she could tough it out for a couple of weeks, her mother would be back home in Chester after the New Year.

A tapping at her bedroom door startled her. Hastily slipping into her dressing gown, she asked, "Who is it?"

"It's okay; it's only me, Dylan."

She sighed and opened the door to allow him access, holding the sides of her dressing gown close together.

"What's the matter?" Her tone was one of annoyance. He'd promised he wouldn't bother her.

"Don't worry; I haven't come to harass you. I just wanted to let you know that I won't be around for a few hours tomorrow in case you are feeling unsafe. I have to pick my mother up from the station, and then I'm taking her to lunch."

"Oh, okay."

"You can join us if you want?"

"Err... no thanks, I think I'll pass. Isn't Cassandra going with you then?"

"No, she's off back to London."

Her heart skipped a beat.

"I told you, Cassandra and I are no longer an item. She has her life and I have mine."

She felt like saying that she'd love to join him and his mother for lunch, but then she feared she'd sound too keen to jump into Cassandra's shoes. After all, she couldn't be sure if the woman wasn't coming back after Christmas.

"Which of course, does leave me a manager short...?"

"You mean me?" she asked.

He nodded enthusiastically. "Yes, I wonder if you could help me out for a few days if we get busy? We have one small wedding party coming here tomorrow afternoon until Boxing Day. There are only eight guests, including the bride and groom, and of course my mother is coming and my father on Christmas day."

"Your mother and your father?" she asked incredulously.

"Yes, you heard correctly. It's my little plan to build a few bridges between them."

"Oh I see. Yes, I'll help you out."

Of course, this meant that they couldn't very well avoid one another now, could they? His little plan was going to work very well.

She reached for the door handle and her dressing gown slipped a little, revealing bare shoulders. Dylan mentally looked her up and down, undressing her with his eyes. He moved towards her and for a moment, she thought he was about to remove her gown altogether. She hoped he would, but instead he picked it back up for her, replacing the silky material onto her shoulders. His touch was electric; she closed her eyes momentarily and waited for him to take her into his arms. But instead, he backed away, making for the door.

"You'll catch your death..." he said as he left the room, obviously not realising the thought he had left her

with. What had the inscription on the mirror said?
"YOU'RE DEAD!"

****

On Christmas Eve morning, Dylan dined alone in his
quarters. He reflected on Cassandra's departure the
previous day. They had parted amicably, each realising
that their relationship had reached the end of the line. He
was a free man. But how was he going to convince
Stephanie that it was all over?

He looked at the sky through the French doors. Slate
grey. A snowy looking sky. Maybe the weathermen's
predictions would turn out to be true after all. He pushed
his kipper back and forth on the plate with his knife. It
was no use; he had no appetite at all. His grandmother
had once told him, "You'll know when you're in love, lad,
because you won't be able to eat or sleep." He guessed the
wise old sage was right.

He poured himself another cup of coffee and sat
gazing into the flames of the log fire. There wouldn't be
time for him to dwell on Steph today; once his mother
arrived the place would be in uproar. She had a habit of
creating a whirlwind in an empty house. Oh, he wanted to
have her near him for Christmas, it was all he had longed
for all his life to be close to his mother. Instead, she had
been some distant glamorous figure whose modelling
lifestyle had taken precedence over a young boy's
happiness. He remembered how she would tuck him up in
bed at his grandmother's home. She'd bend over, stroke
his head, and then leave behind the scent of her perfume.
Gone into the night, not to return again until weeks,
maybe months later. Now who did that put him in mind
of?

He put down his cup and straightened his tie. Time
for reflection over, he picked up his jacket from the back
of the chair and went out the door. He wondered what
Steph was doing right now. She would be safe at the
castle for the time being. Hopefully, Lawrence Black had
no idea she was back in Wales.

The 'Avalon' room had been made up for his mother.
He'd chosen that one as it paid attention to detail,
something that he and his mother loved. It was a very
feminine room with rosebud curtains and matching

25

counterpane. Quite a romantic room with its soft lighting and carved wooden four poster bed. He hoped she'd appreciate it. The views over the green rolling hillside and wooded areas were spectacular. If she looked to the left she might even notice the lake he'd had specially built.

When he arrived at the railway station, his mother was waiting for him, wearing a sable fur coat she'd purchased in Leningrad when she was married to her rich, much-older husband. Under her arm she held her dog, Mimi. Whatever he did, he just couldn't take to the snappy little Peke. It was an absolute menace. She mothered the dog just like it was a baby. Pity she'd never done the same for him.

"Sorry," he apologized. "I should have got here before you arrived."

"There's no need for an apology," she smiled. "The train was early for once." Something had obviously put her in a good mood, he wondered what it was.

"I was going to take you for lunch, Mother..." he began.

"So why can't you?"

"Well isn't it obvious? We can't take Mimi into a restaurant around here, it's not allowed."

She put on one of her sulky faces, lips pouting, eyes downcast, just like a pampered child. "Poor Mimi. Mama can't leave you alone now, can she?" He recoiled as the dog licked her mistress's face.

"Well if you won't leave her with someone, we'd better have lunch in my quarters at the castle."

"Whatever you think best, darling." She kissed her son lightly on the cheek. He felt like wiping it off at the thought of the dog slobbering all over her. Picking up her multitude of luggage, he heaved her suitcases over to the car.

"So what puts you in such a good mood, Mother?" He ventured to ask on the journey back to the castle.

"You're such a perceptive son," she smiled. "I'm sure that's what makes you such a good designer. Your intuition, your creativity..."

"Never mind about me. I asked about you." She had a habit of deflecting the spotlight off herself whenever asked a question she didn't want to answer.

"Very well. If you must know, I'm considering remarrying Donald."

She couldn't have hurt him more if she had driven a wedge through his heart.

He gulped. He couldn't possibly have heard correctly. "Do you mind repeating what you just said?"

"It's quite simple. Donald and I may remarry soon."

He gripped the steering wheel, he needed to focus. This was going to change his plans for a reunion between his mother and father and a chance to get Donald out of the picture once and for all. Donald was a lecherous old trout. Dylan detested the man.

They had married when he was a young boy and sent for him to live with them at Donald's ancestral home in Berkshire. He'd hated every moment at the house. Living up to tradition and Donald's difficult standards had been like being in the armed forces. Up at six a.m. every morning. Meal times had to be adhered to. His own nanny and governess. Even his own pony.

It was such a lonely life. If he had thought that he'd see his mother any more than he had when he was living with his gran—he was wrong. How he had missed his grandmother's home comforts. She wasn't wealthy by any means, but what he lacked in material possessions; he gained in the abundance of the love freely given in the home.

Eventually, he was sent to public school. Only the best for our Dylan. When he turned fifteen, he returned to his grandmother in Wales and vowed never to live with his mother and Donald again. It wasn't that Donald was a bad person, but he and his mother had a standard to live up to. Each one putting on a mask of prosperity and success every day of their lives. Yet, when they removed their masks, what were they left with?

"Dylan. What's the matter?" His mother's voice intruded into his thoughts.

"Sorry. So this remarriage thing, it isn't a foregone conclusion then?"

"No, not at all. I told him I would need time to think it over. I mean, I missed the house."

Charming. So she missed the house and lifestyle too by the sound of it. No words about her missing Donald himself. Maybe that was a good sign.

****

Following a hearty breakfast, Stephanie took a stroll in the castle grounds. It was such an enchanting place. The kind of place that gave comfort in a quiet moment. It was the ideal setting to reflect on the past, present and future. She could see why Dylan adored it here.

She opened a heavy oak door between two walls which led into a small herb garden. At the opposite end was a fountain. Carved into the stone were Queen Guinivere and Sir Lancelot, lovers in another time and place. She smiled as her hand touched the rough etchings.

Further on, she discovered the lake Dylan had told her about. It was about a quarter of a mile to walk around, he said. He had told her of his intention to keep a couple of swans, which would undoubtedly please the prospective bride and groom staying at the castle at the time. Swans, he had told her, mated for life. She watched two of the elegant creatures glide smoothly across the lake and rest on top of the small wooded island in the middle.

She buttoned up her jacket. The weather was getting colder. A far cry from the beautiful summer she had experienced in Italy. The seasons were lovely in both countries, yet different in respect to the quality of colour and lighting. Finding a bench, she settled herself down and stared into the waters of the lake, almost as if they could reveal some wonderful secret to her. What was she going to do about her future? She felt in limbo. Neither grounded nor in full flight, just here in the present time.

It was Christmas day tomorrow and she'd hardly given it a thought. She could go into Cardiff and buy some gifts, she supposed. She couldn't very well join Dylan and his parents for Christmas dinner without having some presents to dole out. Yes, that's what she'd do, take a taxi into Cardiff. *But what if someone sees you and tells Lawrence?* A voice warned her. *Or what if Lawrence himself sees you?* Telling herself that was highly unlikely, she chose to ignore the voice, determined not to let Lawrence rule her life, and went off to reception to phone for a cab.

****

When Dylan and his mother returned to the castle, he left her in her room with a pot of coffee and a mince pie while he went to see the chef to order lunch for both of them. On the way, he passed Steph's bedroom and knocked on the door. There was no answer, so he went to speak to Julienne at the receptionist desk.

"I'm sorry, Meezter Pryce-Jones," she explained in a clipped, Spanish accent, "but Meez Baynham, she left about an hour ago."

Damn the woman. He had told her to stay put. Why did she have to place herself in jeopardy like that?

"Thanks, Julienne. Just let me know when she returns, will you? By the way, do you know where she went?"

"No, she didn't say, Signor, she telephoned for a taxi."

"Okay. Just don't forget to inform me on her return." He'd had enough of headstrong females for one day. After he'd ordered lunch, he was going back to his quarters for a stiff drink.

****

Stephanie strolled through the bustling crowds in the high street. Excited children and harassed adults only added to the atmosphere. She stopped off at a large department store, purchasing a bottle of perfume for her mother: *Springtime*, it was her favourite scent. That should please her. She then went over to the men's department and debated what she could purchase for Dylan. What did someone buy for a person who appeared to have everything? She would have loved to buy him something a little personal, but decided against it. How would his fiancée feel if she presented him with a gold identity bracelet with the inscription, *With Love from Steph* engraved on it?

So instead, she plumped for an attractive paper weight to keep on top of his desk. For his mother, she purchased a Hermes silk scarf and a pair of cufflinks for his father. That was all her Christmas shopping nicely wrapped up. She was about to leave the store when she remembered Matt and Sandy. She could hardly leave them out, could she? They had both been so good to her. She guessed they wouldn't have had much time to do any Christmas shopping with Sandy in the hospital, so she went to the food department and ordered a Christmas hamper. The store said they couldn't deliver it as she had left it too late, so she decided to take it back to the castle and ask Dylan if he would run her to the cottage to deliver it in person.

As she walked down the aisle in the direction of the exit, she saw someone familiar standing by the jewellery department. It was Lucy Clarke, a hostess at Lawrence's club. Lucy appeared busy, admiring some gold chains with the help of the assistant. Steph took her chance and walked past quickly. Just as she passed, the girl turned around.

"Hi Steph. Long time, no see." Lucy must have had eyes in the back of her head. Then she noticed she had been looking in the mirror on the jewellery counter, that's how she must have seen her. Damn, this was the last thing she needed. The girl would surely go back and tell Lawrence.

Stephanie swallowed. She needed to act as natural as possible. "Hi Lucy. Buying some last minute gifts?"

Lucy grinned. "I thought I would treat myself. You're back for good then?"

Not the question Steph wanted to answer. "Only a flying visit. I'm leaving soon."

"Oh, where are you going then?" she said, chewing her gum.

"I'm off to the States for a month," Steph lied and hoped Lucy would fall for it.

"Lawrence has been asking about you, you know…"

"Oh has he?" She tried to remain calm and collected, but she feared that the tremor in her voice would give her away.

"Yes. He was most upset when you took off like that. By the way, where did you say you went to?"

"I didn't" This was getting too much. "I have to go Lucy, have a good Christmas." She rushed so quickly out of the store that she feared the security guard would suspect she was a shoplifter. The weight of the hamper was slowing her down. *Please, Lord, let me get as far away from here as possible…*

Her prayer was answered as she got outside the shop and hailed a passing taxi. She could see Lucy's reflection in the wing mirror as she stood, open-mouthed, on the pavement. At least the girl didn't know where she was staying, but she was bound to tell Lawrence she was back in Wales. Steph felt the bitter sting of tears as she settled herself down in the back of the cab. How foolish she had been leaving the castle. For the sake of a few Christmas presents, she had risked her life.

****

Dylan carefully wrapped the present and slipped it into his bureau drawer as his mother entered the room without knocking—it was a failing of hers—not respecting his privacy. He felt himself flush as she looked him straight in the eye.

"What have you got there then?"

"Oh, just a Christmas present for someone."

"You looked guilty as sin as I walked in, like a little boy who had his fingers caught in the biscuit barrel." She smiled knowingly at him.

He quickly changed the subject before he got carried away and opened up to her. "I've ordered lunch with Chef. Where would you rather eat, here or in the dining room? I can ask Julienne to take care of the mutt, if you want."

"Dylan, would you please refrain from referring to Mimi as 'The Mutt'. I'd rather eat here if you don't mind, then I won't need to ask anyone to take care of her."

"Very well. I'll ask Chef to see that we are served our meals here."

She smiled for a moment, as if she had forgiven him his derogatory term for her beloved Mimi. "I've been in touch with Donald…"

"And?"

"And…he'd like to join us for Christmas dinner tomorrow, if that's okay with you?" She gave her son a pleading look.

"No, certainly not," he said rather too quickly. That would wreck his plan for getting his mother and father around the dinner table with him for the first time in thirty years.

"Why ever not? Don't you like Donald?"

"It's not that," he lied. "It's just that I had a little surprise planned for you and if he turns up it will ruin everything."

31

"Oh, a surprise? For me?" He nodded. She was a sucker for surprises.

"Look, I'll tell you what...how about if he comes here for New Year's Day instead?" He hoped by then his mother and father would get along so well she would completely forget about Donald.

"Yes, all right then," she replied. He could tell that her mind had gone into overdrive as she looked up at the ceiling as if trying to guess what the surprise might be.

He was going to need to have a word with Steph to ask if she could begin her new position as manager, starting with overseeing the wedding arrangements. The small party would be arriving later that evening for the wedding the following day. He was just about to ring Steph's room when he was interrupted by a knocking on the door. His mother looked at him quizzically.

"Expecting company?"

"No." He went to answer, wondering if it was Stephanie returning.

There, standing at the door was his father. What was he doing a day early? He hadn't had time to prepare his mother for this.

"Well, aren't you going to invite me in, son?"

"Yes, of course."

As his father walked into the room, Dylan realised that for the first time in thirty years, Reginald and Daphne were face to face. Dylan stood back and studied the pair as they looked at each other. His mother showed instant recognition, as of course he realised she had seen his father many times on television and in the newspapers, but his father hadn't clapped eyes on her in thirty years.

Reginald quirked an eyebrow. "Forgive me," he said, "I feel as though I should know you. Have we met somewhere?"

His mother straightened and glared at Dylan. "Is this some kind of a joke?" Dylan shook his head, unable to say a word. "Forget about lunch..." she said as she picked up the dog and headed for the door, pushing past his father.

"A fine figure of a woman..." Reginald commented, watching her leave the room. "Yes, a fine filly if ever there was one and such a temper too. Who is she?"

Dylan found his voice. "My mother."

"Oh," was all his father managed to say, then following a pause, "will she be staying over the Christmas period?"

Dylan pursed his lips and nodded. "I didn't tell her either, I'm afraid. I'm sorry. I should have told both of you the other was invited."

"Don't be sorry, son," his father said, giving him a playful slap on the back. "It'll make Christmas all the more interesting."

"Now that you're here, how about joining me for lunch?"

"Yes please, I could eat a scabby horse!"

"Well I can't promise you one of those will be on the menu, but a nice steak with all the trimmings may taste a little better, I think."

The old man laughed one of his huge guffawing belly laughs. It was good to see him so happy.

****

Stephanie laid out her gifts on the bed. These had better be worth the risk. She realised in amongst the confusion, she had forgotten to buy wrapping paper. Maybe Dylan could lend her some? She just hoped and prayed Lucy Clarke wouldn't go to Lawrence with news that she was back home, but somehow she doubted that the grapevine wouldn't get hold of it. Lucy was a terrible gossip, so chances were if she didn't tell Lawrence herself, the jungle drums would start beating soon and sure as eggs were eggs, he'd find out.

She made herself a coffee and lay on the bed, staring at the ceiling. She must have dropped off to sleep as the next thing she knew, the shrill sound of the bedside telephone ringing disturbed her.

"Steph, you're back then. How about helping me out with your managerial duties this evening?" The sound of Dylan's voice started to clear her muzzy thoughts.

"Sure, fine," she replied with a yawn.

"Where did you get to?"

"I did a foolish thing, so before you reprimand me, I know what I did was wrong. I took a taxi into Cardiff for some Christmas shopping. I made a mistake." She omitted to tell him that she had been spotted.

"Why did you do that? I warned you not to go out."
She was shocked by the angry tone of his voice.

*How dare you talk to me this way. It's my life, not
yours.* She took a deep breath forcing out an apology.
After all, he did have a point.

He sighed. "As long as you realise that and don't do it
again."

"What do you need me to do this evening?"

"The wedding guests should be arriving about seven-
thirty. If you can greet them by reception and ask them if
there are any special requirements, diets, sleeping
arrangements, etc. Give them their room keys and then
show them into the dining room for evening meal."

"Okay. Anything else?"

"Not that I can think of for now. But the wedding will
take place at eleven o'clock tomorrow morning, so I'd like
you to attend with me. I like to add any personal touches
and oversee the kitchen and catering staff. Ensure all the
seating plans are in order, etc."

"Okay, I'll look forward to it." How romantic. A
Christmas wedding. When she was a child, she always
wanted to get married at Christmas time. It probably
went back to the days of her grandparents' wedding. They
had been married on Christmas Eve. Grandmother had
told her how when she and Grandfather left the church it
had started to snow.

"Oh by the way…my little plan has already
backfired."

"Little plan?"

"Yes, about getting my parents together as a
surprise. The old man turned up a day early before I had
time to prepare my mother. She was not at all amused."

"I see. That may be difficult for all of you."

"I suppose so. My father's very happy about the
situation. I'm keeping out of my mother's way this
evening. I need to butter her up, though. Any
suggestions?"

"From what you've told me about her, I bet she'd love
a little pampering. How about a facial, massage, having
her hair done, the lot?"

"Good idea. We have a beauty therapist assigned to
the castle. I'll see if I can get hold of her."

"Well, if you can't, I'm available. I used to work as a beautician. As long as you have the necessary products here, I can offer my services."

"Thanks. I'll get back to you on that."

As she put the phone down, she was starting to feel a lot better about things. She had enough here to keep her occupied for time being.

****

Dylan removed the small, velvet box from the bureau drawer. It had taken him ages to choose the perfect present for Stephanie. He had employed the private services of a local Welsh jeweller. The ring sparkled as he held it to the light. The jade-green emerald held a wealth of its own, surrounded by a cluster of white diamonds. He wanted her to be his wife and planned to surprise her on Christmas day after the wedding.

The question was, would she be willing to be his fiancée so soon when his last fiancée had only recently departed? Cassandra was hardly cold in her coffin, was she? He clicked the box shut and placed it back in the drawer, locking it with a small key. Maybe it was a bad idea.

He went in search of his mother and found her sitting in the guest lounge chatting to an American couple who were in the country 'visiting the castles of Great Britain', as they put it. He paused for a moment to take in the scene. She looked happy enough as the couple hung on to her every word, stopping every now and then to give Mimi a pat. His father couldn't have upset her that much, could he?

She turned around, almost as if she realised she was being watched.

"Dylan, come and join us," she said, patting the chair beside her.

The American couple looked faintly amused, as if they wondered what the relationship was between the owner of a 'British Castle' and a charming woman such as his mother, Daphne Hollingsworth.

He sensed the searching question in their eyes and not to disappoint them, smiled and said, "Mother, I have a surprise for you..."

Dylan heard the woman whisper, "Did you hear that,

Howie? It's Daphne's son. How quaint."

His mother sat bolt upright and met her son's gaze. "A surprise for me?"

"Yes, will you excuse us please?" he addressed the American guests. "I have to take my mother somewhere."

The couple nodded and looked at one another in awe, no doubt impressed with Daphne's connection with the castle.

"This had better not be anything to do with your father," she hissed as she walked down the corridor towards the south side of the castle.

"No, Mother. I know better than that now. I just thought I'd make up for things, springing that little shock on you out of the blue just wasn't fair."

"You can say that again!"

"I meant to prepare you, honestly I did. But my father turned up a day too early. He was only supposed to come for Christmas lunch tomorrow. But it looks as if he's going to be staying for some time."

She stiffened up. "I suppose that pleases you?"

"Well, put it this way, I'm not displeased."

She softened a little as he opened the door to the beauty parlour.

"Meet Stephanie, my new beautician cum manager. She'll sort you out."

"If you think I'm going to be bought off for the price of a cheap hair-do, you're mistaken."

Stephanie glanced at Dylan and stepped forward with a smile. "What a lovely dog. May I hold her for a moment?"

Daphne nodded and handed the little Peke over to Stephanie. The dog looked perfectly happy in Stephanie's arms; she was a natural with animals.

"I suppose I could stay for a while. What other treatments can you give me?"

"Full facial, massage, aromatherapy. Here we are— I'll pass you the complete list."

Daphne put on a pair of half-rimmed, gold spectacles and peered at the list. "Yes, I'm sure I can find something here to suit me. I could do with a bit of pampering."

Dylan let out a long breath. A bit of pampering for his mother, that was an understatement. He gave

Stephanie a grateful smile. "Okay, then Mother. I'll take Mimi for an hour or two so you can have the full works." He didn't really have the time, but if it kept his mother sweet and at the castle it would be worth it.

Chapter Four

It was getting late by the time Stephanie finished giving Daphne her treatment. She had let the woman witter on incessantly between a facial, manicure and a hair cut, and now she felt quite exhausted, as if she had given a difficult client two hour's worth of therapy.

Whatever she had given her—it had done the trick. Daphne was pleased with her appearance and looked more relaxed than she had when she first entered the salon. As Stephanie helped her to remove her gown and swept away the excess hair from her shoulders with a large brush, Dylan popped his head in the salon.

"Ready, Mother?" he asked, winking at Stephanie. His mother nodded. "For a moment there, I thought you were someone else. Someone a good ten years younger!"

His mother laughed. "You flatterer, you. Yes, Stephanie has made a great job of it." She opened her purse and handed her a twenty pound note.

"No, really I couldn't…" Stephanie held her hands up in protest.

"Go on, take it…" Dylan urged. "You don't want to offend my mother, do you?"

Stephanie hesitated for a moment.

"Look," said Daphne, whispering in her ear, "I would have had to pay ten times that amount in some of the top salons in London. You've done me a huge favour."

Stephanie smiled and graciously accepted the money.

"Now, where is my little Mimi?" Daphne looked at Dylan.

"She's fine, Mother. Julienne is taking her for a walk around the castle grounds. If you leave through the back door there, you should catch up with them."

Daphne patted Stephanie on the shoulder and left

through the French doors.

"I think you've made a friend for life there." Dylan grinned when his mother was out of ear shot.

"Yes, I found her all right." She picked up a broom and started sweeping up the salon.

"Leave that for a moment, will you?"

Stephanie looked at him and he moved a little closer, so close she could feel his warm breath on her face.

Then she felt his hand reach out, touching the back of her neck as he pulled her closer. *This is wrong, so wrong*, she told herself.

"What's the matter? Why are you tensing up?" He asked his eyes full of concern.

"This isn't right, Dylan."

"Why not? It felt right that afternoon of the wedding."

"It's just...I can't be sure that things are over between you and Cassandra, can I?"

"You have my solemn word," he replied, "that should be good enough for you."

"But I didn't have your word for it that afternoon when we made love. You never told me about Cassandra then, did you?"

His face softened and he smiled. "I'm so sorry. It wasn't my intention to take advantage of you. I care so much about you..." He reached out for her again and this time she didn't freeze, but instead walked into his arms and let him bring his lips down onto hers. This felt good, so good.

His hands ran up and down her spine and loosened her hair slide so that her hair fell upon her shoulders. They found the zip at the back of her dress, stealthily sliding it down, letting her clothing slip to the floor.

"Oh Steph," he murmured, "I've wanted this for such a long time..." His breath came in short bursts as he pressed against her almost naked body. The only thing covering her flesh was a sheer satin slip and lace bra and panties.

"Dylan, is this right what we are doing?" she asked, hoping for reassurance as she fought to control the emotions that threatened to betray her. "I don't know if we should."

"Of course we should. It feels kind of right to me," he groaned, raising the hem of her slip and lifting her up onto the counter. His hands roamed from her ankles up the length of her slip until they found her panties. She quivered beneath his touch. The same touch she'd felt that spring afternoon at the wedding.

His fingers moved inside her slip and found her breasts. She tingled all over as she caught sight of herself in the mirror, not believing how incredibly erotic the image was.

He moved his hands behind her back and unclipped her bra.

"You have the most amazing breasts," he murmured as he brought down the straps on her slip and bra and feasted on them. "They're like a pair of watermelons."

She laughed at his description. He lifted her up and carried her over to the massage bed behind a flowered curtain as she wrapped her legs around his waist.

"Now then, Ms Baynham...what treatment have you come for today?" he asked with a wicked glint in his eyes, "Do you require a half massage or a full one?"

"Full, please," she whispered, as he removed her panties, tossing them across the room.

"I think I'd like to start here..." he said as his hand roamed up her leg and found her wet, warm place. She shivered beneath his touch. Her head was swimming. This felt so naughty. The salon door wasn't even locked, what if someone came in?

He covered her lips with his as he pulled himself on the bed next to her. "I need a little hand, I think..." He smiled sheepishly.

She undid his leather belt and his trouser button, sliding his trousers down. Then she helped him down with his boxer shorts, revealing his erection.

He lay on top of her and her legs naturally parted to allow him access. As he entered her, he stole her breath away.

"My beautiful, Steph," he whispered, as she let out a low moan.

She hungered for him, wanting to give herself completely to him, to feel his very soul dance with hers.

As he thrust inside her, she bucked her hips beneath

his and they kept perfect timing as her pleasure reached fever pitch, like a wave building up and crashing upon the shore. She didn't hold back, she gave herself completely, moving in harmony with the only man she had ever loved.

A low ripple flittered across her stomach, her breathing becoming rapid and shallow. It was happening. She was having an orgasm, and it wasn't just one wave crashing upon the shore, it was wave after wave, until she feared she would die from the very pleasure.

Finally, she found her breath again, let out a little whimper, and whispered, "I love you, Dylan."

He smiled at her and closed his eyes as he shuddered on top of her, all passion spent.

She looked up at him with tears of joy in her eyes, expecting to see him smiling down on her.

Instead he murmured, "I'm sorry…" and withdrew from her embrace.

"Sorry?" she asked, puzzled. Why was he sorry?

"What if you're pregnant?" He adjusted his clothing.

"Dylan, I would love to be pregnant by you." She cried inwardly as she wondered why she'd said that.

Only a moment ago, she had felt safe and closer than she had ever felt to another person in her life. Now he was getting up, dressing himself. What was going on? He hadn't even lain next to her or held her in his arms afterwards. Was he getting up and leaving or was he coming back to tell her how much he had enjoyed the experience?

She was never to find out, as at that moment, they both heard the salon door swing open. He threw her a towelling dressing gown, "Slip into this," he hissed.

The screen was still around the bed. He straightened his tie and went to see who it was.

"Oh, Julienne," she heard him say in the same tone of voice he always used with his staff, "is anything the matter?"

"No, Meezter Pryce-Jones. I was just wondering if I could finish my shift now, I need to get home for Christmas, I have a flight to Barcelona this evening."

"Of course you can. Ms Baynham will take over from you. Have a good Christmas, and we'll see you in the New Year."

"Thank you. Merry Christmas to you Meezter Pryce-Jones!"

The salon door swung shut as Julienne departed.

"I'll be back in a moment, Steph!" Dylan called out.

Stephanie lay there on the bed for a few moments, hardly believing what had just gone on. Was she out of her mind? She could now be pregnant. In the heat of the moment, she had thought she would love to have Dylan's baby, but Julienne interrupting them like that had been like a bucket of cold water thrown in her face. A wake up call. Before she could get involved with Dylan, she needed to get Lawrence Black off her case, once and for all.

Cautiously, she pulled back the screen to find herself alone in the salon. How could he? How could he reject her in this way? She felt cheap, as cheap as she had felt when she was involved with Lawrence. Tears blurred her vision as she scrambled to put her clothes back on and ran back to her hotel room. He had used her and told her he cared for her, just to get his way with her. Lies, that's what it was, he hadn't got rid of his fiancée at all, he was just making hay while the sun shone.

She took a shower and scrubbed herself all over. She wanted no memory of what had happened between them. Then she rang for a taxi, she just needed to escape to sort her head out. She could take the Christmas hamper over to Matt and Sandy's. She wanted to see how Sandy was anyhow.

****

Dylan found the key for the wine cellar. This was an appropriate moment to bring out the champagne. He'd put it on ice and take it with some flowers back to the salon to give to Stephanie. Damn, how he loved that woman. And now she was his. He contemplated taking the engagement ring with him, but thought maybe he would be better off proposing on Christmas day.

When he got back to the salon, he was surprised to find it all in darkness. He tried the door—locked. That was odd. Maybe Stephanie had gone back to her room? He would have only been a couple of minutes but had got side-tracked by the chef who was asking him questions about the wedding tomorrow. He thought there were two vegetarians, one diabetic and five normal meals, but now it turned out there were two vegans, one vegetarian, and five normal meals. He wanted to know how such a mix up could have occurred. Dylan had tried his best to placate the temperamental Scottish chef, but in the end, had walked out on him. Why couldn't he just use his common sense and improvise? Surely, he had been taught to do that when he trained as a chef?

He made his way along the corridor, still clutching the bottle of champagne and knocked Stephanie's door. No answer. That was odd; he could have sworn she had been as happy just now as he was. The only reason he had been a little distracted was because he was annoyed with himself for not thinking about contraception. Although, he would one day love them to have a child, it wasn't what he had planned for his immediate future.

Where could she have gone to? Maybe he should have explained that he planned fetching some champagne, but he'd wanted it to be a surprise.

Then it dawned on him...she probably didn't think he'd cared the way he'd rushed off like that. She was so vulnerable with men. He could have kicked himself for being thoughtless. He prayed she wouldn't be so foolish as to leave the castle. That really would betray his trust. After all, he had warned her. Maybe getting involved with Stephanie was a huge mistake.

Dylan fought to regain his mental composure. His mind had been fogged with thoughts of Stephanie. Julienne had already left the reception desk. Oh no, he had planned on asking Steph to take over after they had their champagne. Now what was he going to do? He had a wedding party arriving in a few hours. He felt let down by Stephanie again. Now who could he ask? Mother, surely she'd help out?

"I'm sorry, Dylan," his mother groaned when he found her in her room, "I have just got to lie down, I feel a migraine coming on. What about your father?"

"Good idea." He grinned and went off to find the old boy. He found him sitting in the bar telling his long stories to the bartender, who appeared to be listening with great interest.

"Dylan, son. Won't you have a drink with your old father?" He tapped his son affectionately on the back.

"Sorry, Dad. I need someone to cover for me on the front desk. The receptionist has gone home for Christmas. Could you do it?"

"Certainly," his father slurred. "I'd love to."

"On second thoughts, I'll find someone else."

"I could do it for you," Jim, the bartender, interrupted. "We've been quiet in here for a while. I could shut the bar if you like, for an hour or two, until you get back."

"Jim, you're a life saver!" Dylan said, handing a bunch of keys to him. "There's a party of eight coming in later, give them these room keys if I'm not back—they're marked up with their names."

"Okay, leave it to me." Jim gave an assuring smile.

Then, when his father was out of ear shot, Dylan whispered, "It'll be a good idea to close the bar for a while to stop the old dog from getting too tanked up."

At least he knew that the place was in safe hands, instead of in the hands of a drama queen mother or a drunken father.

****

"Steph!" Matt blinked as he opened his front door. "What are you doing here? I thought you were safely holed up at the castle?" Had Dylan told him about Lawrence?

"Can't I pay two friends a visit?" Stephanie replied.

"I'm sorry. It's not how it sounds. I'm pleased to see you, of course I am. But when I asked Dylan how you were, he gave me the impression we wouldn't be seeing you over the Christmas period." Dylan had probably said that to explain her absence.

"Sorry, Matt. Don't take any notice of me, I'm just a little touchy this evening. She handed him the Christmas hamper.

"For us?" She nodded. "How kind. Don't stand on the doorstep, come in. It's freezing tonight." She followed him into the warm, welcoming cottage.

"Well, hello stranger!" called out a familiar voice from the living room.

"Sandy!" Stephanie went in to see her friend who was lying on the settee, well propped up with pillows. "I had no idea about your pregnancy until I arrived back in the country."

"Well, you wouldn't have known, being so far away, would you?" Sandy said with a hint of mischief in her eyes. "So what did happen the afternoon of our wedding?" Matt took it as his cue to leave, muttering something about making coffee.

This was going to be difficult. How could she explain about Lawrence Black? She didn't want to worry Matt and Sandy, especially as Sandy had had her own stalker problem the previous year. Not only that, the woman was in the final stages of pregnancy.

She decided to tell her friend an element of the truth. Taking a deep breath, she began, "Dylan and I got it together at your wedding..." Sandy blinked in disbelief. "Don't look so shocked. Afterwards, I did my Cinderella act and left to stay with family in Italy."

There was a pause for a moment.

"But Dylan never told us!"

"No, I didn't expect he would have. You see, he was already engaged to Cassandra."

"Well, knock me down with a feather. I never even suspected. They seemed more like brother and sister to me. No wonder you left, you must have got upset to find he already had a fiancée. He's a dark horse that one!"

"You can say that again..." Okay, it wasn't exactly the truth about why she had left, an altered version, maybe. Then to change the subject, "So how are you feeling?"

"A little tired. I came home this morning and haven't had to do a thing, Matt has been tending to me hand, foot and finger," she laughed.

"Yes, Matt is good like that. So, do you know what you're having? I mean, a boy or a girl?"

"No, we don't. We'd rather have a surprise. At least we know it's not twins! The way the baby has been kicking me, I wouldn't be surprised if it were a little boy. He'll probably turn out to be a footballer!" She laughed.

"Oh, by the way, I brought you both a Christmas hamper, as I thought you wouldn't have much time for shopping."

"Oh Steph, that's so thoughtful of you." Sandy leaned forward and gave her a hug.

"It's the least I could do, you've both been good friends to me. So have you had any visitors?"

"Matt's mother and Doris from the charity shop were both waiting on the doorstep when Matt brought me home this morning. Oh and Matt's friend phoned early this afternoon to say he'll be visiting this evening."

Stephanie racked her brain to think who the friend might be. Dylan was Matt's closest friend since he'd arrived in Wales. No, it couldn't be who she was thinking of, could it?

Sandy continued, "Of course, I was forgetting you already know him. It's Lawrence, Lawrence Black."

Stephanie's stomach flipped over and her head throbbed as though it might burst. Why did he have to invade her life, her mind, her soul?

"Yes, I know him," was all she managed to say.

"What's the matter?" asked Sandy, sitting up. "You've gone as white as a sheet."

"Oh nothing, just my time of the month." Then, "What time will he be arriving?"

"Anytime now. You don't have to go, do you?"

Stephanie rose and stumbled backwards. "No, really...I...have...to..."

"Are you all right?" Sandy tried to stand.

Stephanie steadied herself. "No, please. I'm fine, honestly. Stay where you are."

Sandy settled herself back down, her eyes full of concern. "Steph, you would tell me if anything was wrong, wouldn't you?"

"Of course I would." She was aware her voice had hiked a little higher and hated lying to her friend, but she didn't want to alarm Sandy. Perhaps she had better not leave quite yet, it would look a bit suspicious.

"Stay a while then."

Steph had to admit that it would have looked a little odd if she left right now, she hadn't been inside the cottage more than a couple of minutes. She hoped and prayed Lawrence wouldn't arrive until after she had left.

"No. I can stay awhile," she said, biting her lip.

"Oh good. Come and sit over here. I could do with the company."

Steph did her best to sound cheerful, but there was

no fooling Sandy.

Sandy looked into her friend's eyes, "I can tell there is something worrying you, what's wrong?"

"I want to tell you, really I do, but I don't want to worry you in your condition."

"But Steph, perhaps Matt and I can help you in some way. Is it something to do with Dylan?"

"No, it's not him, well not exactly." Stephanie stiffened as she heard a loud rap at the front door. Before she had a chance to say any more, she heard Lawrence's booming voice as he was let in by Matt. She held her breath and wondered if Matt would lead him immediately into the living room where they were chatting. But instead, she heard the two men's voices die away, and guessed Matt must have taken him into the kitchen.

"You look awful!" Sandy frowned.

"I need to avoid Lawrence Black," Steph blurted out. "Please don't tell him I've been here."

"But Matt might have already told him..." Sandy's voice trailed off.

"Told me what?" Matt said cheerfully, carrying a couple of mugs of coffee in his hand. Behind him, clutching two more mugs, was Lawrence Black. His face changed from a grin to stone when he caught sight of Stephanie. "You two know each other, of course?"

"Yes, Matt, we do," said Steph in barely a whisper.

"Excuse me while I go fetch the biscuits," Matt added, not appearing to notice Steph's discomfort.

Lawrence gave her a hard stare. "It's nice to see you, Steph." His tone was sarcastic as usual. Then he looked at Sandy, "How are you?"

"Not so bad, Lawrence. I feel like I'm going to have an elephant." She patted her stomach.

"That reminds me..." Lawrence said, now smiling again, "I have something for the baby in the car." He left the room.

Sandy looked at Steph. "Is it something to do with him that you're scared of?"

"Yes, I have got to get out of here. Now he knows I'm back in Wales, I'm in danger..."

Sandy grimaced for a moment and Steph didn't know whether it was due to the baby moving or Sandy hearing of her predicament.

"Slip out the back way while he's gone to the car," she advised.

"I could, but it's already too late, he knows I'm back in Wales. He'll find me wherever I am."

"But Steph, it can't be that bad, surely?"

"Believe me, it is, and you're better off not knowing the truth. Lawrence Black is a dangerous man, I'd advise both you and Matt to keep away from him."

"He's offered to be a godfather to our baby..." Sandy's voice trailed off.

"Yes, that would be a suitable term for someone like him—'The Godfather'," Steph said sardonically. "Maybe I will slip out the back door..."

But it was already too late. Lawrence had returned carrying a large black and white panda bear. "The mention of the elephant reminded me of this," he announced as he handed the panda to Sandy.

Matt laughed as he walked in clutching the biscuit barrel, oblivious to any discord in the room.

"Thanks, Lawrence," Sandy said in a falsely cheerful voice. Stephanie hoped she could keep the charade up a little longer. She would hate Lawrence to think she was scared of him. With any luck, maybe he'd leave before she did, but deep down she knew he wasn't going to let her off the hook.

Stephanie tensed as Lawrence picked up his coffee mug and sat next to her. It was too late—now he knew she was back and she felt like a fly trapped in a spider's web.

Chapter Five

Dylan considered taking a run over to the Bay apartments to see if Steph had gone back there. Surely she wouldn't be so foolish? Where could she have gone to? He remembered her saying something about wanting to visit Matt and Sandy before Christmas as she had bought a Christmas present for them. Maybe she had gone there. At least she should be safe if she had.

He was about to pick up his car keys from the drawer when someone knocked the door. He rushed to open it. *Steph!* He let out a sigh when he realised it was the bartender. "Problems, Jim?"

"Err...you could say that." Jim frowned, pursing his lips.

"What's wrong? The wedding guests not happy?"

"No, it's not that. They all turned up and I've given them their room keys and settled them in the dining room for a light snack and coffee..."

"Then what is it?" He was starting to feel impatient; he needed to find Steph to reassure himself that she was all right.

"It's the chef. He's threatening to walk out!"

"The pompous little man." Dylan located his car keys and followed Jim into the lobby and into the guest's television lounge. When he got there, he thanked Jim and shut the door behind him.

"Mr Pryce-Jones, I am not prepared to put up with this a moment longer..." The man was red in the face and had both hands placed firmly on his hips, as if ready for a fight.

"Stewart..." began Dylan, feeling a little calmer, realising he needed to keep his cool and not inflame the situation, "what's the problem?"

49

"I don't have half the things in my kitchen that I need. I cannae be dealing with this. Och, it's sacrilege, man!"

"What is?" Dylan was seriously baffled.

"Well, whoever has been ordering things for the kitchen? I left explicit instructions for what I wanted to make for the wedding guests. Now, on top of that, I find out we have vegan guests too!"

Dylan almost burst out laughing the way the chef referred to vegans as if they were from another planet. "Well, what exactly is a vegan diet, Stewart?"

"No meat of course, like a vegetarian, and no dairy products or eggs. I had planned on making a selection of quiches for the buffet. Now what on earth can I give them?"

Dylan patted the harassed chef on the shoulder. "How about making them one of your marvellous nut roasts?"

Stewart looked as if he was deep in thought for a moment and smiled, "Aye, that's a canny idea and I could whip up a tomato and basil sauce to go with it as well!"

Dylan smiled. "Problem solved. I have to go…"

"Hang on a moment," Stewart grabbed him roughly by the arm, "what about dessert? I can't give them the crème caramel, it contains eggs."

"Fruit salad," Dylan shouted as he rushed out through the door.

"Och, you're a marvel man!" Stewart shouted back at his boss.

And you're a bleeding dickhead, mate, Dylan thought.

****

It was the most uncomfortable half hour of Stephanie's life, sitting in Matt and Sandy's living room on a sofa hemmed in by Lawrence Black. Ever so often, she looked at the wall clock and tried to keep up with the polite, but strained conversation. Finally she said, "Well I'd better be off, lots of things to get ready for Christmas…"

"Okay," Sandy said, smiling at her friend.

"I just thought of something," Matt began, "you came by taxi, Lawrence can give you a lift back."

Before she had a chance to reply, Lawrence was on

his feet and had grabbed hold of her elbow and was ushering her out the door. "Yes, it's no problem for me to drop you off. Where did you say you were staying?"

Sandy heaved herself up from the sofa and tried to intervene. "It's okay Lawrence, Steph can stay here; I'll book her a taxi later."

"I wouldn't dream of it," Lawrence butted in.

"Yes, go on Steph," Matt urged, "you'll have a hard job booking a taxi this time on Christmas Eve." For a moment she considered ringing Dylan, but didn't want to involve him. She needed to get out of this situation and fast.

Before she knew it, she had said her goodbyes to Matt and Sandy and was standing on the pavement outside. As Lawrence opened the car door, she wrestled free from him and sprinted up the road. If she could just make it a little further, she could try to lose him in the bushes up ahead...She heard her own heart beat thumping in her ears as she fought to keep ahead of him. Her breathing became laboured and she glanced behind to see him gaining on her. She was no match for his prowess.

"Think you can give me the slip, you bitch!" He grabbed hold of her hair and put her in a head lock, just like she'd seen him do many times at the club with unruly customers.

"Please, leave me go..." she begged as she struggled to breathe. She felt the pressure on her neck as he squeezed. He had knocked her about in the past but it had never hurt her as much as this. Lawrence released his grip then yanked her hair again so tightly, she had tears in her eyes.

"Leave you go? I'll never leave you go; you know that!"

"I promise I won't say anything," she said, as he marched her to the car.

"I'd never trust a woman," was all he said as he bundled her into the back of the car. She tried to get out, but the car appeared to have some sort of a child lock on. Lawrence didn't have any children, but she guessed he found the lock handy when he was putting the thumbscrew on people he wanted roughed up.

She whimpered like a baby in the back seat,

wondering what he had in store for her. Whatever it was, it wasn't going to be nice. As he started up the engine, she saw Matt come rushing out of the cottage, too late to save her. Sandy must have told him what she'd just confided in her. It was too late for anyone to save her now.

****

When Dylan arrived at the cottage, he was surprised to see Matt speaking to two police officers on the doorstep. He worried for a moment that something had happened to Sandy and the baby.

As he got out of the car, Matt came over to meet him.

"I'm so sorry," he said, hugging his friend.

"Sorry? For what?"

"Steph was here earlier. If I had realised for one moment, I would never have let her get in the car with him."

"Matt, slow down. Who are you talking about?"

"Lawrence, Lawrence Black."

Dylan groaned—his worse nightmare was becoming a reality.

"How long ago was this?"

"About an hour since. You see, she confided in Sandy, when I was out of the room making coffee that she was in danger. She wouldn't say too much about it as I don't think she wanted to alarm Sandy, due to her condition..."

"And?"

"And Lawrence turned up while she was here. I didn't notice anything strange, but Sandy said that Steph looked petrified the whole time he was here. Of course, I made things worse by suggesting he give her a lift home. Sandy filled me in on what Steph had told her as soon as they were out of the door. I went running outside to stop her going with him. I was about to make an excuse, like saying I needed help to get Sandy to the hospital as her contractions had began, but by the time I had got outside, he was driving off."

"So you phoned the police?"

"Err, not exactly. They called around as they are seeking his whereabouts. It seems he's wanted for questioning regarding a missing woman. One of the residents at the Bay mentioned my name when they questioned them. They remembered I stayed at his apartment once when he was away overseas."

"I knew about the murder, but not that the police were after him."

"Murder?" Matt asked, with a puzzled expression on his face.

"It must be the same person who has apparently gone missing. Steph told me she was in danger because she saw him strangling a woman. Her apartment at the bay overlooks his."

"Yes, I know that only too well," Matt smirked, "the first day I moved into his flat, she told me she could see me coming out of the shower! But I shouldn't smile, this is serious isn't it?"

"Yes. Matt, I have to find her. Where do you think he's taken her?"

"Well, I doubt if he would have gone back to his apartment, the place is probably teaming with police. In all honesty, he could have taken her anywhere."

Dylan felt his heart sink. If anything should happen to her, he would die.

"Think, Matt. Stephanie's life is in danger!"

Matt frowned for a moment and said, "Well, if it's any help to you, he owns two night clubs in Cardiff, 'Night Zone' and 'Freak Out'. Both clubs are at either end of the city, 'Night Zone' is fairly up market, attracting business men, etc; 'Freak Out' attracts a younger clientele. Hang on, I have a couple of flyers he left here recently, the addresses are printed on them."

"Thanks, mate." Dylan watched his friend return to the cottage. He deliberated whether he should go talk to the police who were sitting in their car parked down the road. He remembered what Stephanie had said about not contacting them. He would need to do a little detective work for himself.

"Here they are," said Matt, handing them to him, a little out of breath.

"Do me a favour, will you?" Dylan took the flyers out of Matt's hand.

"What's that?"

"Don't mention anything to the police about Stephanie being with Lawrence. She warned me not to contact them."

"I haven't said anything so far. Just that he was here earlier and had already left. I thought I'd check things out with you first."

"Good. And that's how I want it to stay."

"You have my solemn word. Don't forget to keep me informed if you hear of anything or if you need any help."

"You'll be the first to hear anything. Now get back inside to that lovely wife of yours."

As Dylan walked down the path he felt a shiver run the length of his spine. What if it was already too late? It may be like looking for a needle in a haystack.

****

"Stay down in the back!" Lawrence commanded as he drove off at speed. "I'm warning you, bitch, if anyone sees you; I'm going to kill you!"

Stephanie lay down and tried to control her breathing. The main thing was she needed to keep her cool if she wanted to stay alive. She had to find a way to elicit his sympathy and keep in communication with him. "Shall I hide under this blanket next to me?" She asked, hoping that her trembling voice wouldn't give away how frightened she really was.

"Yeah, that's a good idea," he said, using a softer tone of voice.

It was cold anyway, so she drew the blanket over her and felt a little more secure. She wondered where he was taking her.

About a quarter of an hour later, he broke sharply and swore, hitting both hands on the steering wheel.

"The bleedin' cops are here!" he yelled.

"Where?" She asked, wondering if she dare risk sitting up to look out of the window.

"Surrounding the Bay apartments. They must have been questioning Danny King at the club, I bet he shopped me." Danny King was one of his henchmen. Steph knew him from the time she worked for Lawrence. Lawrence had never fully trusted him but had kept him on as a favour to his father, Jack 'The Knife' King, one of the well-known, East End of London, gangsters from the 1960's.

Lawrence reversed the car and drove off at speed.

"Where are we going?"

He looked at her in the driver's mirror, "I've just thought of the perfect spot." She tried looking at his reflection as if to gauge what sort of a mood he was in. She could have sworn that he had smiled.

He drove for a few minutes, then stopped the car. They were at the marina. He got out of the car. Stephanie tensed as Lawrence released the lock on the car door and hauled her out into the night air.

"You're hurting me!" she cried, desperately hoping that someone could hear her. There was no one else around. The only sound was Christmas music drifting from an apartment behind them.

"Now listen to me," he said, roughly grabbing hold of her arm, "I'm not in the mood to be pissed about. You say nothing and do nothing to attract attention. Got that?" She nodded.

He walked her towards a set of steps. It was hard to see exactly where she was going, so she took each step tentatively. Relief flooded over her when she finally reached the bottom. They were standing next to a large cruiser.

"Yours?" she asked.

"No, it belongs to Father bleedin' Christmas. Who do you think it belongs to?" he replied sarcastically. "Bought it as a Christmas present to meself. The good thing is, no one around here knows I own it." He gave a sneering laugh and then pushed her towards the awaiting boat.

"Where are you taking me?" she asked, searching his eyes for any kind of response. All she saw was contempt in them. How could someone she thought she had loved so much be so cold hearted? What had made her fall for a man like him in the first place? The break from him had somehow made her view him now as he really was—a man with a heart of steel, with no compassion for anyone or anything.

"My dear, Steph," he taunted, "the police are on my case. I have to get out of the country."

She swallowed. "Wh...where to?"

"Ireland," he answered as if it was only a bus stop away.

"But what if I say I don't want to go with you?" she said defiantly.

"You have no choice. How do I know that I can trust you not to tell the police I supposedly murdered someone?"

"Because I've kept your secrets in the past, haven't I?" She challenged.

"That may be so, but this is different. You think I murdered that woman, but I didn't..."

"I know what I saw, Lawrence. You had your hands around her throat."

"Like this?" He grinned as his hands closed around her own throat.

For a moment, she thought she would see her life pass in front of her eyes as he pressed tighter and tighter. Was he going to kill her? What made him so violent? This was the man she had once loved; now all she could see was pure hatred in his eyes. She struggled for breath as he maintained the pressure. She brought her hands to her throat, desperately trying to prise his hands away. It was no use; she didn't have the power or the energy to fight him. She was going to die.

Slowly, he released his grip and once more she could breathe freely. Then, she burst into tears.

"I'm sorry," he said, taking her into his arms. "I shouldn't have done that. Not to you. I'm sorry I scared you. That girl you thought you saw me strangling, Jenni, worked at my club. She was my top hostess, but she started to double cross me. She wanted a cut from my business. Yes, I did have my hands around her throat and squeezed so hard that for a moment, I thought I had killed her. She just passed out and when she came around, I pushed her out through the front door and haven't seen her to this day."

Stephanie massaged her sore neck. Could she believe what he was saying? He had lied to her in the past, but only about his business dealings.

"So, if you haven't done anything to her, why are the police chasing you?" She fought to regain her composure.

"That, my dear Steph," he said, lifting her chin and looking into her eyes, "is the million dollar question. She was reported as missing by her family a few months ago. I think the police may have found her body."

Stephanie was almost beginning to feel sorry for him

until she thought back to the death threat scrawled in lipstick on her mirror.

"What's the matter?" Lawrence asked, his eyes now full of concern. Had she misjudged him?

"Nothing." She looked at the floor.

"Good," he said, as he guided her towards the awaiting boat.

****

Dylan stopped his car—he needed time to compose himself. He had to have a minute to think what to do next. He needed a plan, he couldn't just do nothing. He had to visit Lawrence's clubs to quiz his staff about his whereabouts.

He decided on a whim to take someone with him, so that it would look as if he was a punter on a night out. Now who could he take? His father, maybe? Or Jim? He decided his father was probably the best bet. Jim was needed at the hotel and at least as his father had been drinking, he already looked like a business man on a night out.

"I must say that's very nice of you taking me for an evening out," his father said when he got back to the hotel.

"Now, listen," Dylan warned, as if dealing with a child, "this is very important. I need to get some urgent information. All I want you to do is to act the part of a drunken business man and you won't need to do much acting."

"Pardon?" his father blinked.

"Stephanie is in danger. I need to find her, Lawrence Black has taken her. He's a shady character involved in allsorts of underworld activities including drugs. I need to visit a couple of his clubs to question his staff."

"Won't that be dangerous?" Reginald asked, looking and sounding a little more sober.

"Probably. But don't you worry about that—you can leave the worrying to me."

"I don't like the idea of that. Let me take a shot gun with me..."

"Don't be so silly, man. We can't walk into one of his clubs with a shot gun."

"Suppose you're right." His father shrugged. "Just

take heed, son. From what I know about the drug scene and other organized activities, you need to be particularly careful. I'll watch your back for you."

Dylan smiled to himself at the thought of his sixty-year-old, inebriated father coming to his defence. Then his smile turned to a frown when he realised he was about to walk into the lion's den.

****

Stephanie climbed aboard the cruiser, aptly named, 'The Seafarer', with Lawrence inches behind her.

"Don't look so worried." He smiled as she turned to face him. "Just enjoy yourself!"

She couldn't believe her ears. He had just kidnapped her and he was expecting her to enjoy herself. The man was unbelievable.

She had to admit the boat was the ultimate in extravagance. No expense had been spared. It was wall-to-wall luxury with expensive limed oak fittings and leather upholstery. As well as having a decent galley kitchenette, the boat also had its own bar.

"Very nice," she muttered, "but I should be getting back. I should be working this evening."

"And how, my dear, did you manage to get a job so quickly?" he asked as he stroked her cheek.

She recoiled from his touch. So Lucy Clarke must have told him she had spotted her in the department store.

"I fell in lucky, I guess." She knew she wasn't fooling Lawrence for a moment. He was fishing. He wanted to know where she was working and with whom she was staying.

"Don't give me that bullshit, Steph. Someone is helping you." He grabbed hold of her shoulders and shook her. "Who is he? Anyone I know?"

She started to sob again and he released his grip and let his hand rest on her shoulders. This was so confusing. One moment he was Mr Angry, the next he was Mr Nice Guy; but that had always been Lawrence's way—keeping the enemy guessing.

"Not to worry. It will all come out in the wash," he said, heading for the door and locking them both in the boat. He took the key and put it in his trouser pocket.

"Now, what will you have to drink?"

She glanced at the large clock on the wall in the shape of a ship's wheel and trembled. It was five past six; she would be late for her shift at the castle if he kept her much longer. Dylan would think that she had run out on him. That was the last thing she wanted him to think. Her stomach turned over. It would probably be too late to get back in time for work, she'd just as well take a drink to take the edge off her anxiety. She knew it wasn't the best way to go about things, but for the situation she was in, it might be the only way out. "I'll have a gin and tonic," she said, hoping he wouldn't detect the quaver in her voice.

"Gin and tonic?" Lawrence raised his eyebrows, "I always thought you were a shandy girl, three shandys and you're anybody's." He laughed at his own joke, then trailed his fingers down her arm, lifting her hand and kissing it.

Stephanie felt a shiver, it wasn't cold on the boat; it was just the memory of being Lawrence's 'bit of stuff'. How could she have cheapened herself? The man epitomized evil.

****

Dylan parked the car and he and Reginald walked the short distance to 'Freakout'. The place was bouncing as loud rap music vibrated out onto the street. A large queue of young people stood outside, shivering, waiting to get in. It looked an exclusive club. Two bouncers walked the length of the queue and picked the people they wanted seen inside. They appeared to pick out only the good looking girls and smartly dressed boys.

"We'll never get in here," his father said, ready to walk away. "Besides, I look too old. I'm more mutton than lamb these days."

"Just a minute," Dylan smiled. He walked to the front of the queue, "watch this..."

He whispered something in the manager's ear and the black-suited man smiled and waved both men in.

"What did you say to him?" Reggie asked, bemused.

"I pulled my, 'You're in the presence of a Famous Fashion Designer' card." Dylan winked.

"Oh!"

"Yes, it's that sort of club. They want to attract celebrities. Charlotte Church and Gavin Henson frequently come here."

His father looked suitably impressed. "Well, if it's good enough for them…"

When they got inside, his father headed straight for the bar. "Hang on a moment," Dylan said sternly, pulling his old man by the lapels of his jacket. "We haven't come here to enjoy ourselves!"

His father straightened his jacket and looked his son squarely in the eyes. "Get real," he said, "we have to make it look as if we are a couple of punters."

"Okay, I'm sorry. Get yourself whatever you like and get me a soft drink."

Dylan was amazed to see his father buy two apple juices. He winked at Dylan. "It looks like whiskey. Of course I realise we have to have our wits about us. We have to look the part don't we?"

Reginald got into deep conversation with the barmaid and Dylan went for a walkabout. He glimpsed a man in a white shirt and black trousers coming from an office, leaving the door slightly ajar. He glanced around to ensure he wasn't being watched and swiftly entered the room. It appeared to be the manager's office, by the comfortable furnishings and silver plated photographs on the large, imposing desk. He yanked open a filing cabinet and rifled through some files, but there was nothing of interest, they appeared to be invoices mostly.

He spotted a safe in the corner, pity he couldn't get into that.

Men's voices echoed down the corridor, so he hid behind some large cardboard boxes.

"Black's gone into hiding," he heard a man with a Cockney accent say in a condescending tone as he entered the office. "Stupid bastard, he's got police flocking all over the place."

"Where do you think he's gone?" asked the second man.

"I think he'll try to get out of the country somehow. Trouble is all the airports and ports will be on alert."

"Suppose he could go underground for a while until this mess is sorted out. How do the police know Jenni is dead anyway? They haven't found a body."

"Believe me, I know she's dead. She fucked about with Black once too often for her own good."

"He killed her?"

"Nah. I did." The hollow laughter of both men hit Dylan like a kick in the guts. What kind of monsters were they? And more importantly perhaps, what kind of a monster was Black?

****

Stephanie found that the drink was starting to go to her head. She had to find a way to get Lawrence drunk, but stay sober herself. If only she could get her plan to work.

"What's the matter with you?" he barked.

"Just thinking..."

"Oh yeah. What about?"

"Christmas," she lied.

"Spending Christmas with that poncy designer fella, I expect." He spat out the words.

So, he knew that she and Dylan were an item, did he? But how? Maybe he had seen them slip away to the bedroom at Matt and Sandy's wedding.

"Do you want another G & T?" she asked. For a moment, she feared he would say no, as he hesitated. She breathed a sigh of relief when he nodded his head. Now was her chance. She poured a good slug of gin into his glass and very little tonic. Into her own, she poured tonic only.

She handed him the glass, tentatively. He took a sip and started to cough. "You couldn't have made this any stronger for me," he growled. She froze and then he started to laugh. "To you're very good health!" He lifted his glass and drank it all in one go. "Aren't you going to drink yours?" She took a sip, wondering how many glasses he would need to drink before he passed out. She had a feeling he would need a lot more and maybe a little help from his medicine cabinet.

"I have to go to the ladies' room." She smiled politely.

"Not so fast," he said, pulling her back down next to him, "you won't be able to escape..."

"I'm not trying to."

"Good. Because you and I have some unfinished

business in the bedroom little lady. You're going to give me my Christmas present tonight!"

If ever she needed help it was now. She hoped and she prayed he had some sort of medication in his bathroom to knock him senseless.

Chapter Six

Dylan finally heard the two men leave the room and when he was quite certain they had gone, he clambered out from behind the boxes and went in search of his father.

The middle-aged man was laughing and joking with the girl behind the bar. For a split second, Dylan considered staying at the club a little longer, until he noticed a man standing by a pillar gazing in his father's direction.

Deciding they'd better make a quick exit, he grabbed hold of his father's arm.

"C'mon old boy, we'd better get out of here. You've had enough to drink!"

"But I've only been drinking apple juice," his father protested.

"I know," Dylan whispered, "you're being watched."

Reginald accompanied him out of the club, jostling through crowds of rowdy youngsters. When they got outside into the fresh air, Dylan sighed a breath of relief.

They were just about to walk to the car when a booming voice shouted after them, "Hey, wait a minute!"

"Run," Dylan ordered, both men sprinted towards the car.

"Stop!" the voice shouted again. This time it sounded nearer. The man was gaining on them. Dylan turned to glance behind him. It was the same man who had been watching his father.

Suddenly, a hand grabbed his shoulder.

"What do you want?" Dylan asked between breaths. His father was already doubled up, fighting to get his breathing under control. Dylan hadn't remembered running so fast since sports day at public school.

"That old geezer..." the man said, pointing to Dylan's father, "he's been chatting to my girl friend!"

"He doesn't mean any harm," Dylan explained.

"Asking her questions..." the man continued.

Reg finally found his breath, "Look, if it makes you feel any better, she told me absolutely nothing."

"I know," the man said in a softer tone. "She knows nothing. But I know—you can talk to me."

****

Stephanie scanned the bathroom for anything she could find to put in Lawrence's drink—anything that might knock him out for an hour or two—giving her time to escape.

She tried opening the bathroom cupboard, but found it was locked. She wondered why and guessed he had a stock of recreational drugs to supply to people stashed away in there. He never took them himself—he said that's why he was so successful. Once suppliers started taking them, they were on a slippery slope downwards.

Finding nothing there, she decided on a different tack—to check his kitchen cupboards.

"I'm hungry," she announced, sitting down next to Lawrence.

"Afterwards, babe," Lawrence smiled, running his finger tips up and down her arm. *Afterwards will be too late.*

"I need something to sustain me."

"Go make us both a couple of sandwiches. There's a loaf of bread and some ham in the kitchen."

She hurried off in the direction of the kitchen. It would be an ideal opportunity to route around.

"Don't forget the brown sauce for me!" he called after her.

You'll have more than brown sauce if I have my way.

Pulling the bread out of the cupboard and the butter and ham from the fridge, she put them to one side on the counter. Quickly, she searched the cupboards and drawers for any sign of painkillers, sleeping tablets, anything to knock the brute out. But there was nothing, the only thing she could find was some laxative powder at the back of the drawer.

"Hurry up and get back to me," Lawrence called from

the kitchen.

"Won't be a moment!"

She switched the kettle on and made two cups of coffee and emptied some of the powder into one of the cups and carried a tray with the food and coffee to where he was sitting.

"I could do with this," he enthused, grabbing hold of a stack of sandwiches, eating ravenously.

"I made us some coffee too," she said, sitting down next to him.

She watched him munching away, hoping he would take a slug of coffee, but he didn't. Instead, he stood and poured himself another drink. "Want one?" She shook her head.

"What about your coffee?" she asked.

"I'll leave it—you have it."

"Look, if you're going to take this boat to Ireland, you're going to need to stay awake..."

"You're right as always," he smiled, picking up the wrong coffee.

"That's mine," she said, taking it out of his hand. For a split second, he looked at her, his eyes like slits. "No sugar, remember? I've put two spoonfuls in yours." His face relaxed and he picked up the other cup and drank it. What if he could tell by the taste? He didn't appear to notice anything untoward.

"Coffee okay?" she asked.

He nodded and when he had drained his cup she offered him another one. Maybe this was chancing her arm, but she had to make him as ill as possible, she reasoned.

"Okay, I'll have another. Once I've finished, we'll have a little evening delight in the bedroom and then we're on our way."

Please start working, she thought to herself as she brought him a second cup laced with laxative powder. But it didn't seem to be having any affect on him at all. She didn't know how long it should take, but she knew she was running out of time.

Once he put his cup down, he grabbed hold of her and kissed her. He smelt strongly of a mixture of alcohol and expensive aftershave. She wanted to wretch. His kind of love wasn't real love. Lawrence was a taker. The love she had with Dylan was real, wasn't it?

He grabbed hold of her hand and pulled her towards the bedroom. Opening the door, she could see that it was a den of seduction. The ceiling was mirrored and animal print fur throws and cushions were liberally dispersed across the king sized bed.

Peeling off all his clothes down to his boxer shorts, he stood like an Adonis, upright, proud of his physique. Whatever she thought of him, he had a well-toned, tanned body. He worked out regularly at the gym and looked after himself. Physically, a catch for any woman, but emotionally, a monster of depravity.

"Now, get your kit off!" He smiled as he sat down and patted the side of the bed next to him.

"Put some music on and I'll perform a striptease for you," she offered nervously.

"Baby, that's what I love to hear," he said, switching on the built in hi-fi above the bed.

She danced around seductively and slowly, taking her time as she removed her cardigan, allowing it to fall to the floor with great aplombe. Then, teasingly, unbuttoning her blouse.

She didn't need to remove anything else as Lawrence appeared to go into some sort of a spasm, moaning loudly, doubling up on the bed like an adult foetus.

"What's wrong?" she asked, her voice full of mock concern.

"There's something wrong with my guts!" he groaned. He got up suddenly from the bed and staggered towards the bathroom, clutching at his stomach as if his life depended on it.

She picked up his trousers from the floor and rifled through his pockets for the key she had seen him put in there earlier.

She started to shake when she realised it wasn't there. What had happened to it? She knew he'd put it in his pocket. Then, she felt something hard under her foot—the key. It must have fallen out when he'd taken his trousers off.

Putting her blouse and cardigan back on, she headed quietly for the door, clutching the key tightly in the palm of her hand. It was her passage to freedom. Whatever happened, she didn't want him to catch her leaving, so she carried her shoes in the other hand.

When she reached the exit, she slipped her shoes back on and inserted the key in the lock. It easily turned and she pushed the door, but she couldn't open it. It was also bolted. She struggled to slide the bolt across, but it wouldn't budge and her fingers kept slipping. She wiped her sweaty palms on the side of her jeans and gave it all the strength she could muster, finally sliding the bolt open.

She slipped out through the door and locked it with the key behind her. At least he wouldn't be able to run after her in a hurry with the stomach cramps and without his key.

A sensation of pure relief flooded through as she stepped outside in the cold night air once more. She thought she heard a faint banging noise coming from inside the boat as she gingerly made her way up the steps and back on to the quayside to freedom.

****

"Right, tell me all you know," Dylan commanded, sitting in the back of his car with the man, his father keeping a look out in the front.

"Haven't we forgotten something?" the man said, holding out his empty palm. Of course there had to be some sort of a catch, didn't there?

Dylan pulled his wallet out of his jacket pocket and dropped a twenty pound note into the man's outstretched hand.

"Go on," he urged.

The man kept his hand out, so Dylan dropped another twenty pound note in to his palm. When there was no reaction; he dropped another and another, until the man accepted the money.

"Okay..."

"This had better be good," Dylan said through gritted teeth. He hated people who were on the make.

"It is. Black didn't kill Jenni. It was Danny King, one of his henchmen."

That would tie in with what he heard when he was hiding in the office. One of the men had taken the responsibility for killing the girl as if it was something to boast about. Another notch on a ganster's belt.

"Then why are the police looking for Black?" Dylan asked.

"Because that's what King wants them to think—it deflects the spotlight off him."

"If it isn't a silly question—then why did King kill Jeni?"

"She knew too much of King's involvement with Black's illegal activities."

"So you'd say that he's a dangerous man."

He nodded. "Extremely dangerous. I think that's why King wants him in the frame. He's worried about his own neck."

The bloke clicked a button on his watch to illuminate the time and sighed as if he should be elsewhere.

"One last question. If Black was going to hide out— where would he go?"

"I couldn't possibly tell you that." The man's eyes widened as if he was fearful of passing on any more information to them.

Reggie leaned over from the front seat and dropped something in the man's lap.

"It's a Cartier," he said, "Better than that old thing you're wearing, worth a bob or two…"

The man let out a low whistle. A beat then, "I've heard that he's just bought a cabin cruiser. It's moored down at Cardiff Bay. It's called the 'Sea something' or other…"

"Aren't they all," said Dylan sardonically.

"Let me think…"

"Come on," Dylan urged.

"I got it, 'The Seafarer'." Realising he had his thirty pieces of silver, the man left as abruptly as he had arrived.

"Thanks for that, Dad," Dylan said, patting his father's shoulder. "If you hadn't parted with that Cartier watch, we may never have known about the boat."

"What Cartier watch?" his father replied innocently. "It's a cheap copy I got down the market."

"Then we'd better get out of here sharpish before he realises," Dylan said, getting into the front of the car.

****

When Stephanie reached the quayside, she ran as fast as she could. She had visions of Lawrence exploding with anger when he found out she was missing, and of him getting even angrier when he realised he was locked inside his own boat.

What if he had another key?

She hadn't considered that. If that were the case, then in moments he could be gaining on her. She was too far away to run back to the castle and had very little money on her.

There was a call box nearby. She dialled Matt and Sandy's number, but it was engaged. How inconvenient, now of all times. Then she tried contacting Dylan at the castle, but Jim, who must have filled in for her at reception, answered saying that Dylan had gone out for the evening with his father. So, she was right about Dylan—he couldn't have cared much about her all along— if after their love making session he had just gone out on the town with his father.

Now what?

She had exhausted her options. She didn't want the police involved. The only thing she could do was return to her flat.

****

It was like looking for a needle in a haystack, there were so many boats at the marina. It was hard to read the names in the dark.

"Over here," Reggie shouted, "I think I've found the 'Seafarer'."

Dylan looked in the direction Reggie was pointing, "No, that says 'Seacruiser'!" he cried in exasperation. "You could do with some new glasses, Dad."

"Sorry," his father muttered.

Dylan's voice took on a softer tone. After all, his father was only trying to help. "It's okay," he said, "it's hard to see anything in the dark here with only a few lights."

Dylan returned to the car for a torch he kept in the boot for emergencies. He feared they would never find the cruiser. Wearily, he trudged on, desperation allowing him to continue with his quest. Then he stopped, staring at what would be at least the tenth boat they had checked. He blinked with exhaustion as his eyes focused on the name, 'The Seafarer'. His heartbeat increased as he and his father approached the boat. A light burned in the cabin window and he thought he detected movement...the sound of banging was coming from inside.

Dylan went down the steps and knocked. No one answered, but someone knocked back to him. Perhaps it was Stephanie?

"Hello!" he shouted. "Is anyone there?"

He heard a low groaning noise, sounding like some sort of a wounded animal. That wasn't Stephanie. On second thought, it sounded like a man, obviously in some sort of distress.

"Are you all right?" Dylan called out.

"No. I think I need help. I'm locked in and I'm not well." If that was Lawrence, then he sounded like he was at his wit's end. Just as well, Stephanie must have managed to get away from him. He breathed a sigh of relief as he felt his heart beat return to normal. Steph had somehow managed to get away from the monster.

****

Stephanie let herself into her apartment. The place smelt musty—unused. If she could just lie low here for a while until she could get through to Matt or Dylan, then she would be safe. But her instincts told her that it was the first place Lawrence would think to look for her. There was only one thing for it. She had to find some cash, phone for a taxi and get back to the castle.

She rifled around in drawers and cupboards, trying to rack her brains if she had any spare cash around the place. All she could find was the left over Italian currency she had brought back with her. Maybe she could phone for a taxi anyway and ask someone to pay her fare either back at the castle or at Matt and Sandy's? The trouble was that Dylan might still be out enjoying himself and Sandy could easily have gone into labour by now.

Time was of the essence. She picked up the phone and dialled a local cab firm she had used in the past, but she was told they were booked up for the next couple of hours due to it being Christmas Eve. She looked at the clock and trembled from top to toe as she imagined

Lawrence breaking down the door of her apartment, to get to her. Tentacles of fear gripped her as she imagined him bearing down on her, his hands around her throat. This time not letting go. Her mouth became dry and beads of perspiration formed on her brow.

She dialled Matt and Sandy's and this time Matt answered. "Steph, thank goodness you're okay. We've both been worried about you."

"Matt, thank heaven you answered this time. Where have you been?"

"We had a false alarm with Sandy and I put her in the car to get to the hospital, but then her so-called contractions stopped. She said it must have been those false ones women sometimes get. Branston Kicks."

If she hadn't been in such desperate need, she would have laughed there and then. "You mean Braxton Hicks. I'm at my Bay apartment. I managed to give Lawrence the slip from his boat at the marina. I laced his coffee with laxative powder and escaped when he was taken ill. I've locked him in but I'm frightened he might escape and come after me."

"Stay where you are. I'm coming for you," Matt commanded.

He didn't wait for a reply...all Steph heard was the buzz of a phone line that had gone dead.

Sometime later, she picked up a half-opened packet of cigarettes and lit one. She badly needed the nicotine to soothe her frazzled nerves. She was only a social smoker, but it was at a time like this that she was desperate for one.

How had her life become one big mess?

Only a year ago, she had it all going for her. Good job in the city, her own car and Bay apartment. Now she was jobless—unless she included her temporary position as hotel manager—, carless, and the way her finances were going, she would soon become flatless too.

Inhaling deeply, she let out a long plume of smoke. It had only been ten minutes since she had spoken to Matt, so he would need at least another ten or fifteen minutes to get to her.

And then what? If she went back to the castle, would Dylan be angry with her for not doing her shift? Would he believe what had happened to her? Why, oh why did her mother have to be away now of all times?

Hearing a car pull up outside, she glanced out the window tentatively, relieved to see it was a young couple being dropped off. One thing she knew for certain, she would never have the same security in the apartment—it would never feel like home again.

****

"Black, is that you?" Dylan shouted angrily.

"Yes," he groaned in reply.

"Have you got Stephanie in there with you?"

"No, the bitch has gone and locked me in, done a runner after she poisoned my guts with something."

Dylan hesitated for a moment. If Black was really on his own, then he may be better off leaving him locked in the boat and calling the police. But no, Stephanie had been adamant—no police. He could phone someone at the club to go fetch him: Danny King or one of his other cronies, perhaps?

But what if he was lying and Steph was still on the boat with him? That was hardly likely was it?

"I'll get you help," he called to the man and left the quayside with the banging sound ringing in his ears.

"Why did you leave him there?" Reg asked.

"Because, my dear father, it's safer to leave him locked in than it is to have him on the loose, trailing Stephanie. Besides, when I've found her, I'll ring his club for someone to help him."

"Good thinking, son," Reg said, giving Dylan a slap on the back. "Now where to?"

"I think," said Dylan, "we'll pay a little visit to the Bay apartments."

****

Twenty-five minutes went by with still no sign of Matt. Stephanie lit another cigarette. What if something had happened to Sandy and he was on his way to the hospital instead? Or what if he had been involved in an accident? Or what if... There were no more 'what ifs'. Relief flooded through her when she heard a car draw up outside. She let out a long breath. Thank goodness for that. A knight in shining armour had come to her rescue.

****

When they arrived at the apartment, all was in darkness. Maybe Stephanie was playing it safe so Black wouldn't realise she was in there. Dylan placed his thumb on the intercom buzzer and waited for her to answer. He tried a second and a third time, but there was no response. He reasoned that maybe she was afraid to answer in case it was Black himself. He spoke into the intercom hoping and praying she would hear his voice, but there was no reply. He buzzed one of the other occupants, who sounded a little suspicious, but came to the front door in any case.

The man hiccupped and swayed as if he had been indulging in too much of the Christmas Spirit.

"Stephanie Baynham, you said?" Dylan nodded and the man scratched his head.

"Good looking, around five feet, ten inches, looks a little Italian..." Dylan explained.

"Yeah, I know who she is," the man gave a little smile that indicated as well as realising who she was, he didn't half fancy her. It was good that he knew her at least, now maybe they would get somewhere. "But I haven't seen her in months. She disappeared quite suddenly. I thought she had moved."

Reg whispered in Dylan's ear, "Ask about the caretaker!"

"Have you got a caretaker around here?" Dylan persisted.

"Yeah. Grumpy old bugger he is and all. Albert Evans, he lives in that ground floor apartment opposite. You should find him in."

Dylan thanked the man and went in search of Albert. If they could just gain access to the flat then he could see for himself if she was there or not.

Albert Evans opened the door, his brows drawn together in irritation. An old black and white movie played loudly on the television behind him. His stained vest and messed up hair gave the impression that he hadn't bathed or changed his clothes in days. The smell of stale perspiration made Dylan want to gag. What was a man like him doing in charge of upmarket apartments for goodness sake?

"Look, what authority do you have to ask me to check

the flat out?" he moaned.

"Miss Baynham's life could be at risk. I just want to check she's okay. I could always go to the police and ask them to get a search warrant."

Albert's eyes opened wide. "No, no, there's no...no... need for that," he said, stumbling over his words. "I'll just fetch the master key."

Dylan and Reg searched every room in Stephanie's apartment, but there was no sign of her. He was just about to leave when he spotted a half smoked cigarette in an ashtray on the coffee table. He picked up the stub, it was stained with pink lipstick. The smell of smoke still permeated the air. So she had been at the apartment, but where was she now?

He got his mobile phone out of his pocket and rang Jim on reception at the castle. No, Jim hadn't seen her. He rang Matt, Sandy answered and told him that Stephanie had rung them and Matt had gone to fetch her over half hour ago. He hadn't returned yet.

That would be it then, she was on her way home. He let out a long breath—thank goodness, she was safe.

****

Stephanie eagerly opened the car door. "Matt, thank goodness you got here—" She froze. *King!*

"Relax, Steph. I'm not going to hurt you," He glanced across from the passenger seat. "I'm just concerned with Lawrence Black's whereabouts?"

"Look, I was expecting someone else," Stephanie protested to the driver. She chided herself on being foolish to have opened the car door without checking the driver was Matt. How was she to have known that Danny King had the same model car?

She let out a long breath. That was a relief, she wasn't being kidnapped again; but the question was, should she trust King and tell him where Lawrence was? Or should she say nothing? After all, Lawrence had said he didn't trust King himself.

No matter how much she disliked Lawrence, she didn't want any harm to come to him.

She leaned in through the open door. "I haven't seen him." Her mouth felt dry and she hoped she sounded convincing.

"Are you quite sure, my lovely?" King sneered.

"Y...yes. To be honest, I've been avoiding him since I got back home. In any case, how did you know where I was?"

"I didn't. I heard you were back. Seeing you was purely coincidental. I was on my way to Black's apartment when you got in the car. I knew it would be the last place he'd go to ground with the police swarming around the area, but I was passing this way on my way to check out his boat."

Stephanie swallowed. Some coincidence! She had a feeling he was up to something and maybe it involved herself and Lawrence too. So if he went to the boat he would find Black. "No, I haven't seen him at all," she persisted.

"Well if that's the case, little lady, I'd better drop you off enroute. Now where did you say you were going?"

"I didn't. I'm booked into a hotel in Cardiff," she lied. King reached over and dragged her into the passenger seat. She screamed but knew it was unlikely anyone could hear her. "Really, there's no need to give me a lift—" But it was too late as he leaned over and pulled the door shut, then used his electronic key to lock all doors and windows.

"Of course I need to give you a lift, Steph. You don't know who is about this time of night." He threw his head back and laughed.

Stephanie swallowed. She had to keep her head clear. There was no way she was going to tell him she was staying at the castle. She hoped this wouldn't be a repeat of what happened with Lawrence earlier in the evening. But she needn't have worried, he dropped her outside 'The Globe Hotel' in Cardiff, at least she could hail a taxi, if she was lucky, back to the castle. She needed to ring Matt and Sandy to explain what happened. She waited until she had reassured herself that Danny King had driven off before walking into the hotel to find a telephone. It was his way of warning her he could take her at any time.

****

Dylan and Reg walked towards their car, when a silver Mercedes drew up alongside them. There was something familiar about it. *Of course, Matt. What is he doing here?*

Matt wound the window down. "I got a call from Stephanie about three quarters of an hour ago. She wanted a lift. Where is she?"

"We meet again." Dylan smiled at Matt in the driver's seat. "Sorry, mate, she isn't here. I knocked earlier and I even got the caretaker to open her flat. She's been here; there was a cigarette butt in the ashtray, so she couldn't have left long ago."

Matt furrowed his brow. "But why would she leave when she knew I was coming to pick her up?"

Dylan had a sickening feeling in the pit of his stomach. Black couldn't have got to her, because he was locked in the boat when they left him. Where was she? That was the million dollar question.

Chapter Seven

When Dylan and Reg returned to the castle, it was almost midnight. Soon it would be Christmas day. Dylan asked Jim if Stephanie had returned but the bartender shook his head.

"Fancy a drink?" Dylan asked his father.

"I wouldn't mind a brandy after the night we've just had," Reg replied.

"And what sort of night have you just had?" Daphne stood in the doorway behind them, arms folded. "You both look the worse for wear."

Dylan considered telling his mother the full story, then thought better of it. "We just had a little too much to drink, Mother, that's all." He smiled.

"Pull the other one," his mother said, raising her voice. "Now him, I can quite believe that of." She pointed at Reg. "But Dylan, you're not a big drinker. Now, is someone going to tell me what on earth is going on?"

"It's Stephanie, Mother. Earlier this evening, she left the castle unexpectedly and she appears to have gone missing."

"You didn't have an argument, did you?" It was evident his mother had really taken to Steph.

"No, of course not. I've since found out that she went to visit our friends, Matt and Sandy. But she was given a lift afterwards by Lawrence Black."

Daphne raised an eyebrow. "And who is Lawrence Black?"

"A local business man who's into a bit of this and a bit of that. A very dangerous character by all accounts."

"So you think she's with this Black person right now?"

"No, we know she's not. He's locked in his own cabin

cruiser at Cardiff Bay."

Daphne sat down. "This is all getting too much for me to take in, Dylan."

"I know it's confusing," began Dylan, sitting on the arm of his mother's chair, "but I'm concerned about her. I've discovered that she went to her apartment at the Bay, but no one knows where she is right now. I became even more concerned when I ran into Matt. He'd turned up to give her a lift after she phoned him, but she wasn't there when he arrived."

"I see." His mother cleared her throat. "You obviously care a lot about Stephanie," she said, looking into his eyes.

"I think I'd better phone the police." He skilfully changed the subject. Of course he damn well cared about Stephanie, but for now he wasn't comfortable telling his mother. Not until he was absolutely sure that Steph reciprocated his feelings.

Daphne stood. "I suppose you have no choice," she said, pouring brandy from a decanter on the sideboard into three crystal tumblers.

She handed one to Dylan and the other to Reg. For a moment, Dylan noticed his mother and father locking eyes. What were they thinking? The spell was broken as Jim knocked the door.

"Miss Baynham's outside in the corridor. Come quick, she doesn't look very good."

Dylan's heart flipped at the mention of her name. Thank goodness she was back. He found her sitting white as a ghost in a chair in the lobby. He knelt down beside her and took her icy hands in his.

"Are you all right, Stephanie?"

She raised her head to look at him. The sparkle she had in her eyes earlier that evening, when they had made love was gone. Now her eyes looked dead. She was badly traumatised, that was for sure and he knew who to blame, didn't he?

"Yes, I'm all right, thanks. I just had a bit of a shock that's all."

"Come into my quarters and I'll get you a brandy." He helped her to her feet and led her into his private rooms. He nodded towards the door to indicate to his parents that he wanted to be on his own with Steph. They obligingly left, closing the door behind them on their way out.

Stephanie gulped down the amber fluid and sat in a comfortable armchair by the fire. "Thanks. That's better," she said, the colour returning to her face.

"What happened to you? I know that Lawrence Black forced you into his car..."

"It was awful, Dylan. I was sorry I left the castle in the first place. I just wanted to take the Christmas hamper over to Sandy and Matt."

"I know," he said, sitting down opposite her.

"Lawrence Black showed up at Matt and Sandy's. He offered me a lift home. I tried to run off when we got out of Matt and Sandy's but he ran after me and caught me by my hair and bundled me into his car. It had child locks in the back so I couldn't escape." She took a few breaths. "Then he took me to the quayside at the Bay and forced me aboard his cabin cruiser."

"I know. I called to Matt's looking for you. I got some info about the boat from someone at the club. We did manage to find him, Steph."

Stephanie raised her eyebrows. "You did?"

"Yes. He was banging on the door of the boat when we arrived. We left him in there. I've telephoned his club for someone to let him out."

"So you went to all the trouble of looking for me?" Why did she look surprised? He didn't get it at all. Surely, she understood after their love making session just how much he cared about her?

"Yes. I went over to see Matt and he told me what had transpired. He tried to come after you when he realised what had happened, but it was too late. He gave me the name of Black's clubs, so my father and I went to investigate. I found out some interesting information, too."

"Oh?"

"It wasn't Black who killed Jenni. It was Danny King."

"How did you discover that?"

"I overheard King talking to another one of Black's henchmen at the club. I was hiding in the office."

"I feel awful now, Dylan, accusing Lawrence of the murder."

"Yeah, well don't feel too awful about things. Remember he tried to kidnap you this evening."

She frowned. "I guess you're right and if I hadn't laced his drinks with laxative powder, I might not be sitting here right now, but on my way to Ireland."

So that was why Black had sounded unwell on the boat. It was starting to make sense. "And I'm so glad you're not," Dylan said, patting her hand. "Now I think it's time we both got to bed, don't you? We have a wedding to attend in the morning." If Stephanie hadn't been through such a traumatic ordeal, he would have suggested she sleep with him in his bed. His heart raced as his love for her swelled. It took all of his will power to allow her to return to her own room.

****

Dylan accompanied Stephanie safely back to her room. She toyed with the idea of asking him about earlier in the afternoon, after their lovemaking session. Why had he gone cold on her? Maybe he was treating her like a one night stand? Is that how men saw her?

"Do you want me to fetch you something to eat?" he asked. He used a master key to open the bedroom door.

She shook her head. "No, thanks. I'll just make myself a cup of hot chocolate and then I'll hit the hay."

"Make sure you get your glad rags on for the wedding tomorrow," he said as he was leaving. "Oh and by the way…"

This was it, he was going to apologise for his earlier behaviour and tell her how much he loved her.

"Yes?"

"Merry Christmas, Steph."

Her mouth felt dry and she swallowed hard. "Merry Christmas to you, too," she whispered and went inside her room so he wouldn't see her crying.

What had she done? Coming back to Wales had been a huge mistake. She should have stayed in Milan with her grandparents. Almost every man she had ever known had used and abused her and Dylan was no different from the rest. Yet, hadn't he gone to all the bother of looking for her earlier that evening? When she'd thought he'd been out drinking with his father, he had actually been out looking for her, concerned for her safety.

She filled the kettle in the bathroom and caught sight of herself in the mirror. She looked horrid. There were dark circles beneath her eyes and her skin looked pinched. She needed a good night's sleep before the wedding tomorrow. Someone else would have the chance to tie themselves to another person for the rest of their lives. Thankfully, it wouldn't be her.

As long as she lived, she would never trust another man. If they were going to use her, she was going to use them. No way was she going to fall for all that love crap. She had told Dylan she loved him after they had made love, giving herself to him wholeheartedly, yet, he had been cavalier with her heart, tossing it aside.

She drank her chocolate, cleaned her teeth, got undressed for bed and fell into a fitful sleep dreaming of being hunted down by some man in black. The words, 'You're Dead' appeared in blood on the walls of her bedroom. She woke up and switched the light on. No, it was just a dream, there was nothing on the wall. Anyhow, why should Lawrence want to kill her? It wasn't him who had murdered Jenni, it was King.

****

Stephanie awoke to the sound of hushed voices outside her bedroom door. Then someone tapped on it.

"Come in," she said, sitting up, yawning and stretching her hands above her head.

A tray appeared through the door, carried by Dylan.

"I thought you might appreciate this after your ordeal last night."

She nodded and smiled as he set down the tray of coffee, toast and eggs.

"What time is it?"

"Nine o'clock. I thought you could do with the rest."

"But I must get up and get dressed, what about the wedding?"

"It's all under control," he said, pouring her a cup of coffee from the pot. "There's no need for you to do anything for now, just turn up at eleven o'clock in the Camelot Room for the service. The reception is being held afterwards in the small banquet room."

"You're so good to me." She smiled.

"Oh, I almost forgot...I have a present for you."

He reached into his jacket pocket and pulled out a small package wrapped in gold paper and tied with a red ribbon.

For a moment, she thought it might be a ring. But why? Why would he want to give her a ring? He had made his feelings obvious yesterday when he had abandoned her right after they'd made love.

She held her breath as she untied the ribbon and tore into the small package, her heart beating wildly beneath her silk nightdress. So loudly, she feared he might hear it.

"Do you like it?" he asked, a broad grin appeared on his face. He had such a lovely smile.

She stared at the silver brooch, fighting the disappointment. Why was she so let down? She was finished with men anyway, right?

"It's lovely," she said without looking into his eyes, but the tremor in her voice must have given her away.

"Have I upset you?" He sat down on the bed next to her. "I'm sorry, I didn't mean to."

"It's not that..." Her vision blurred with unshed tears.

"Then what is it?"

She took a deep breath, "It's what happened yesterday between us."

His eyes softened but before he could respond, his pager went off. "Sorry Steph. It will have to wait. I'm wanted in the kitchen. I expect Chef is having a hissy fit again about something or other. We'll talk later, okay?"

She nodded and he bent down and kissed her on the top of her head. When he had gone, she looked at the brooch again. It was quite nice, really. Maybe not as personal as a ring might have been. It had a silver Celtic design with a green emerald in the middle. She would wear it for Christmas dinner in the evening.

In any case, if she had been disappointed with this gift, what would he think of hers? A paper weight for his desk—that was hardly original was it? She would have liked to give him something a little more personal, something that would have really meant a lot to him. But she hadn't wanted to give the impression that she cared as much as she did.

Thinking back to her relationship with Lawrence had made her realise what she had with him was borne out of fear and not out of love. Fear and love did not go together. Everything she did or said in his presence was controlled. If she said the wrong thing, he gave her one of his evil stares. If she did the wrong thing, the consequences were even worse for her.

In the early days, he had been sweetness and light. She had felt like herself then, her self-esteem still intact. But as the weeks and months passed, she lost her sense of self as almost all her ideas and comments were laughed upon or sneered at. Her confidence sunk to an all time low. But that wasn't all. The prodding began. If she stepped out of line, there was the odd push here, the odd slap there, and then that fateful night when he had overstepped the mark.

She had arrived home late from a Christmas shopping trip with her mother. She had told him she would be back by six pm to make his dinner, but she had missed the train. Arriving much later than she had planned, she stood outside the door of his apartment with the sound of her heartbeat thudding in her ears. She thought of all sorts of excuses: the trains were cancelled, she'd left her shopping behind and had to go back for it, she'd had an accident...but the simple truth was she had been enjoying her mother's company so much that she had forgotten the time.

He had been waiting for her as she opened the door. He dragged her by the hair, sharp pain shot through her head as tears sprung to her eyes. "Bitch!" he shouted. His hand came out, slapping her cheek so hard, she recoiled. "How many men were you with tonight, whore?" He dragged her to the bedroom, where he ripped off her skirt, tore at her tights and panties, prised her legs apart and raped her.

Afterwards, she had lain on the bed staring at the ceiling, sore between her thighs, wondering how she could escape her life, her man...

The strange thing was, he didn't appear to have realised he had raped her. He got out of bed and said, "Good girl—don't do it again, will you?" She shook her head and as he made her a cup of tea, she buried her face in the pillow and wept.

Later, she showered vigorously, washing the blood from her nose, and then applying ointment to her bruises. She would scrub all traces of him from her body, even if she couldn't scrub him from her mind.

"Put some make up on those bruises when you go to work tomorrow." He had commanded and she had. No one was to know. It was to be 'their little secret'. One thing about Lawrence—he didn't like others to think badly of him. He was a charmer.

At least Dylan didn't treat her that way. Maybe he had been thoughtless to have left her after their lovemaking without another word, but whatever she said about him, there was no fear of him, just a little fear of abandonment.

****

Dylan went to check on his parents on his way to the kitchen and was surprised to see them having breakfast together in the dining room, talking animatedly with one another. Their voices died down as he approached.

"So are you all set for Christmas dinner this evening?" he asked.

"Wild horses wouldn't keep me away!" Reg guffawed.

"As long as I don't get one of my headaches," his mother groaned, holding her hand up to her temple.

"For goodness sake, Mother. Don't you think you could make it without a headache for just one night of the year?" Dylan surprised himself with the vehemence in his voice.

"Dylan, don't speak to your mother like that." His father intervened.

"Yes, well I do have good cause. You weren't the five year old child who cried himself to sleep night after night because his mother had left him yet again to take another modelling assignment in London, were you? Neither were you the young teenager who needed his father!"

He turned his back on the both of them and walked out of the dining room before he said anymore. Maybe he was wrong to vent his anger on them. Okay, they had both let him down badly in the past, but it was Christmas day in the here and now and he needed to remain calm for the wedding.

If the truth were told, his anger had little to do with his parents. He was angry with himself for not being man enough to get down on one knee and ask Steph to marry him. If she said no, then at least he would know for sure. All he would be left with was wounded pride. Yes, that's what he'd do, propose to her this evening and give her the ring.

It was a chance he needed to take. He had loved her from the first moment he had set eyes on her at one of Sandy's dinner parties. He had already heard bad things about her, but when they spoke to one another, he felt like he had met a kindred spirit. At first, it was only he who could see the good in her, but eventually she had made amends to Matt and Sandy for her behaviour. Little by little, they had come around to trusting her, realising that she was only a frightened little girl beneath it all.

Dylan had known about Lawrence Black from Matt, but he'd had no idea that Stephanie had been involved in any of his activities and he doubted that Matt had known the extent of Lawrence's world. Matt was a down-to-earth trustworthy guy. No way would he have let Steph leave with Black if he had for one moment guessed what he was up to. Matt had lived overseas for years, so he had been clueless about Black's recent activities. When had Lawrence changed? He must have been a decent guy at sometime, surely?

He went into the kitchen to find out what Chef's problem was. He'd almost forgotten about being paged with his little outburst towards his parents.

When he got there, he found Chef amongst a cloud of steam.

"I cannae be having this mon," the little man said, wiping the sweat from his brow. "We're shorthanded in here. I'll never get it all done in time."

"Relax," reassured Dylan, laying his hand good-humouredly on the man's shoulder.

The chef's voice went up an octave as he became more wound up then ever. "How can I relax? There's vegetables to be peeled, puddings to be made. I have Christmas lunches to prepare as well as the wedding reception."

"Don't worry." Dylan smiled. "I have two able assistants who can come to the rescue."

****

Stephanie took a shower and put on the most suitable outfit she had for a wedding—a red woollen dress. She plucked a flower from the arrangement on the coffee table and attached it to her dress with a pin. Should she wear her hair up or down? It didn't really matter, but she didn't intend letting Dylan down. Deciding to wear it up, she secured it with a large hair slide. She slipped on a pair of black, suede court shoes, picked up her clutch bag off the bed, and she was ready to go to the wedding.

When she arrived in the banquet room, the small assembly of guests were already seated, so she sat at the back of the room. The registrar stood at the front behind an ornate desk with the wedding register and fountain pen ready for the happy couple to sign. Piped Celtic music played softly from an overhead speaker. Where was Dylan? Surely he should have been here by now? She glanced at her watch. There were only a few minutes to go until the ceremony started.

Something was amiss, she was sure of it. Ever so often, she glanced at the doorway to see if the bride and groom or Dylan would come through the heavy, panelled door. Finally, she held her breath as Dylan entered. The guests turned around, obviously expecting to see the bride and looked disappointed, their faces falling as they realised it wasn't her, but the owner of the castle.

"Stephanie," Dylan hissed. He motioned toward the door and she followed him outside the room. His face was pinched, his brows drawn together.

"What's the matter? Have the bride and groom done a runner?" She laughed.

"Actually, you are quite near to the truth. The bride is refusing to marry the groom."

"But why? How?"

"It seems they had a quarrel last night and she's not sure she wants to go through with it. Will you speak to her, please?"

"Me?"

"Yes. She's on her own. I found her crying outside.

I've already reassured the groom that I will do my best to get her to the ceremony."

"So that's why he was looking so edgy sitting down the front."

"Yes, he's the only one who knows about this. He hasn't told the other guests."

"Well the best thing is if you can stall them for a while, and I'll talk to the bride. I'm not sure I'll be of any help, mind you. What's her name?"

"Maria. Thanks, Steph. Just do your best, please. Otherwise I am going to have eight unhappy people here on Christmas day."

Stephanie gave him a reassuring pat on the shoulder. "By the way...what happened to your parents? I thought they would have been attending the wedding."

"I've roped them in to help with the Christmas lunches. Chef has been complaining again."

Stephanie smiled to herself, thinking of Daphne with her sleeves rolled up in the kitchen. It was a wonder she hadn't had one of her headaches that Dylan had told her about.

****

Stephanie found Maria sitting by the lake watching the swans. Her hair and make up looked like they were ready for her big day, but she was dressed in a pink, zip-up sweat shirt and matching pants. At least there were some signs she had intended getting married if she had gone to the trouble of having her hair and make up done.

Maria managed a little smile as Stephanie came up close. "Do you mind if I sit next to you?" Stephanie asked.

"No, it's a free country." Maria must have thought Stephanie was just another guest. Maybe it would be a good idea if she kept her thinking that.

"Are you just here for a Christmas break?"

"Yes and no. I mean, it's supposed to be my wedding day." There was no mistaking the catch in her voice.

"Oh?"

"Yes. I should have been getting married about now." She put her hands to her face and started to sob.

Stephanie undid the clasp on her clutch bag and passed Maria a tissue. "Here," she offered.

"Thanks. I'm sorry to cry like this in front of you."

"That's okay," Stephanie said as gently as she could. "Are you sure it's too late for you to get married?"

"Yes. I had a row with Joe, my fiancé, last night. We never got around to making it up. He probably hates me now."

"Was it over something serious?"

"No. It's just I was a bit annoyed when he got drunk with his father and uncle in a pub down the road when I thought he should have been with me."

"But isn't it traditional for the bride and groom to be separated the night before the wedding anyhow?"

"That's what my mother said. She said I should learn to be less selfish if I want to keep Joe in my life. But I can't help it, I'm so insecure you see. I fear he will meet someone else."

"And has he ever shown signs of wanting to be with someone else?"

"No. He's the complete opposite, he's very loving and attentive..."

"But?"

"But I was engaged to another man three years ago. At first it was all wine and roses, but afterwards we moved in together and he started staying out late, making excuses, that kind of thing. I found out a couple of months later from a friend that he had been seeing another woman behind my back. The strange thing was, he still wanted to marry me but I feared he would do it again, so I called it a day. My worry in this relationship is that once I marry Joe, he may do the same thing to me."

"Yes, that's understandable. I think I would feel that way too. But Joe isn't your last fiancé, so it's not fair to compare him with someone who cheated on you, is it?"

Maria turned her head and looked Stephanie in the eyes for the first time. "I guess you're right—it has been unfair of me."

"You know, you won't get over these feelings overnight. I suggest you see a counsellor, either with Joe or on your own, otherwise you'll be bringing old baggage into a new relationship."

"Yes, I can see that now. Thank you."

"That's all right. How about I take you inside and fix your make up and then you can go ahead and marry Joe?"

"Believe me, I'd like to do that, but it might be too late."

"Trust me, it's not. I was sent out here by Mr Pryce-Jones, the owner of the hotel to have a word with you. I'm the new manager, Stephanie Baynham." Stephanie liked the sound of that.

"Oh, I didn't realise."

"Why on earth would you? You haven't seen me before. I'll just ask Mr Pryce-Jones to delay the guests a little longer, he can give them a glass of sherry or something while I fix your make up. I used to be a beautician."

Maria smiled and wiped away a tear. "You're an angel, Stephanie." She had been called many things before, but never an angel.

****

Dylan wondered how much longer he could keep the guests waiting for the bride to show up. He had already got his mother and father to bring in some trays of sherry to offer around and the music was changed to some Christmas music to set the mood. He could do no more than that.

It was now twenty five minutes after eleven. He noticed the registrar glance at his wrist watch once or twice. What if he had to be somewhere else? Then the door opened and Stephanie walked in while heads turned and whispers went around the room. She held a thumb up to Dylan and smiled as she took her seat.

What a clever girl. He felt like hugging her, but this was neither the time nor the place.

He cleared his throat. "Ladies and Gentlemen, this is the moment you have all been waiting for. We apologise for any inconvenience caused. Will you all please be upstanding for the bride."

The music changed to the 'Wedding March' and Maria stood gazing up at her father, who was waiting in the doorway for her, ready to escort her to her groom-to-be's side. Seeing the look on Joe's face as he watched Maria walk down the length of the red carpet, past smiling guests, made this moment all worthwhile. Yes, he believed in love. Yes, he believed in marriage, and yes, he believed it would be right for him to propose to Stephanie tonight.

"Ladies and Gentlemen…" the registrar began, his once cold expression replaced with a warm smile, "we are gathered here today to witness the marriage of Joseph David Hamiliton to Maria Helen Whittaker. Marriage should not be entered into lightly, or without due thought, but with respect and with the intention of sharing in each others' happiness…"

For a moment, Dylan felt a lump in his throat as Stephanie gazed in his direction. Was she feeling what he was feeling right now? It was impossible to tell for certain. All he knew was that it felt so right to him. When she had gone missing last night, he knew for the first time in his life that he couldn't live without her. Didn't want to live without her. If anything had happened to her when she was with Lawrence, it would have cut his heart in two.

But now here they both were, safe and sound. There was nothing or no one to get in their way.

Finally, there was the exchanging of rings, "I give you this ring as a symbol of my commitment to our marriage. I promise to love, cherish, honour and respect you, from this day forward, for better, for worse, in joy and in sorrow, in sickness and in health, for as long as we both shall live."

Dylan glanced over at Steph and the words spoken took on a special meaning for him.

The couple was pronounced man and wife by the registrar. Dylan thought he saw Stephanie wipe a tear from her eye as the couple kissed. Despite what had gone on earlier, they looked so happy together, as though they were meant to be.

He felt the sudden urge to go to his quarters, get the ring and take Stephanie somewhere quiet to ask her to marry him.

"Meet me down by the lake in a few minutes," he whispered to her.

She smiled and a puzzled look swept over her features. "Why?"

"There's something I need to say."

"Oh, okay," she replied, still wearing a confused expression.

He got back to his room in double quick time and in his eager anticipation, struggled with the lock of his walnut desk. There it was, the velvet box. He opened it and stared at the emerald. He hoped she'd love it; he'd had it created just for her.

He slipped the box into a pocket on the inside of his jacket and made for the lake.

"Mr Pryce-Jones!" a voice called after him. He turned around to see Jim, out of breath behind him. "I've been looking everywhere for you."

"What on earth's the matter?" Dylan asked, irritated that he was being held back from his mission.

"It's the police. They want a word with Miss Baynham."

It would probably be about Lawrence kidnapping Stephanie last night. "Okay, no problem. I'll take them to her. Go back to reception, Jim." Dylan glanced in the direction of the foyer and saw two officers, a male and a female, standing side by side.

"Detective Sergeant Dawn Hunter," the female officer introduced herself, "and this is, D.C Miller. I understand that Stephanie Baynham is staying here as a guest with you?"

"That is correct."

"Can you please take us to her?"

"Come this way," Dylan led them down the corridor and out through the double French doors past the herb garden and towards the lake. At last Lawrence Black was going to get his comeuppance.

****

Stephanie sat on the bench overlooking the lake in the same spot she had sat less than an hour since. Funny, that moment now seemed a lifetime away. She embraced herself to keep warm, rubbing the palms of her hands against the sleeves of her dress, all the while wishing she had brought a jacket with her. The sky was a dove grey colour and a bitter wind nipped her ears and nose.

What on earth did Dylan want to see her out here for? Granted it was a lovely setting with the swans and all, but it was far too cold to be out of doors for too long. Was he going to thank her for helping to get the bride to the wedding? Or was he going to apologise for abandoning

91

her after their love making session? Was it only yesterday afternoon? That too, seemed a lifetime away.

She heard voices and spied Dylan striding towards her. Who were those two people walking a few paces behind him? Had something happened? He had a strange expression on his face, his brow heavily creased with concern.

Dylan sat down next to her and held her hand. "We'll have to postpone this meeting for another time," he whispered. "The police want to talk to you. I think it might be about your kidnapping last night."

She was genuinely puzzled. Who had told them? "But I haven't reported it to the police, Dylan. How could they possibly know?"

Dylan raised an enquiring eyebrow. "The only thing I can think of is that Matt might have got in touch with them."

"Maybe you're right."

"I'll tell you what, I'll make a pot of coffee and you can speak to them in my quarters."

Stephanie was just about to agree when the police woman stepped forward with a stern expression on her face. "Stephanie Baynham?"

"Yes, that's me." She smiled.

"I am Detective Sergeant Dawn Hunter. I am arresting your for the murder of Lawrence Black. You do not have to say anything but it may harm your defence if you do not mention when questioned something which you later rely on in court. Anything you do say may be given in evidence..."

Chapter Eight

"What on earth are you talking about?" Dylan
demanded. "This has got to be some kind of a mistake."

Hunter said nothing, just dangled a pair of silver
handcuffs in front of her.

"But...I...I don't understand," Stephanie stammered,
"Lawrence was alive when I last saw him. I only gave
him..."

"Ssh," warned Dylan, "don't say anymore until I get
you a good solicitor."

Stephanie nodded. The policewoman cuffed her and
she was led to the car, flanked by both officers.

How could this have happened so quickly? One
moment Dylan had been happy and ready to spring into
action by proposing to the woman, and now moments
later, she was being led away by the police. Of course she
hadn't murdered Lawrence Black; he had been still alive
when he and his father had visited the boat. The only
thing he could kick himself for was that he hadn't seen
the man face to face to verify that it was him. Two
questions sprung to mind: how was Black murdered? And
more importantly, who had killed him?

Another strange thing was, how did the police know
to question Stephanie? How could they possibly have
known she was on the boat with him last night?

The only person he could come up with was Danny
King. There was obviously no love lost between the two
men and King had murdered before. He'd heard him
confess it with his own ears.

*Right, pull yourself together. Stephanie needs a good
solicitor.*

Walking into the kitchen, he found his mother and
father having a tot of cooking sherry. His father had a

ruddy complexion and his mother wore a Christmas hat crookedly on her head. Any other time, he would have enjoyed a scene such as this. They were obviously getting on famously with one another.

"Dad!" Dylan pulled his father to one side. "I need your help."

"Wassa matter?" asked his father. Dylan steadied him. The alcohol fumes made him want to vomit. "How can I help my little boy?" Oh no, he needed some solid, sound advice and his father was at this moment, off his trolley.

"Never mind," Dylan muttered under his breath, returning to his quarters to make a private call to Matt.

Matt was helpful but sounded shocked to hear that Lawrence was dead. "I know a good solicitor," he said when he had digested the information. "Warren Parker, lives in Newport. I'll give you his number, but I can't guarantee he'll be around with it being Christmas. Failing that, the police will have their own duty solicitor."

"Sorry to sound so sharp, Matt, but I need someone good."

"Believe me, Warren Parker is the best around these parts, but he doesn't come cheap."

"I don't care, Matt. I'll pay whatever it costs. Even if it means me selling this castle to do so."

"Oh?"

"You sound surprised?"

"I am. I didn't realise that Stephanie meant so much to you."

"Well, she does. I love the woman."

"I can tell that. I'll tell you what, I'll ring Warren for you myself and I'll get back to you a.s.a.p."

"Thanks, mate. I owe you one."

"Don't thank me yet. Let's see if I can locate him first."

Dylan put the receiver down and fumbling in his jacket pocket, checked to see if the ring was still there. He unlocked his desk and placed it back inside. He hoped he'd get a chance to bring it out again soon.

****

Stephanie stood trembling at the front desk of the police station.

"Is there anyone you would like notified that you have been taken into custody?" The custody officer asked.

Stephanie shook her head. Her mother was still in Scotland and Dylan already knew, so who else was there to be told?

"I understand you already have a solicitor sorted for you. Mr Warren Parker, from Parker and Hamilton in Newport."

That was news to her, but Dylan had promised he would sort it for her. She nodded gratefully.

A female officer took her to a room to search her and then led her down a long corridor. The sight of numerous cells with open bars, made her shiver. She had never been anywhere like this in her life. The officer unclipped a set of keys from her leather belt and unlocked the door. Stephanie looked at her for confirmation. Was she really expected to go in there? The officer nodded and give her a sharp prod, until she was inside. She was beginning to feel like a piece of meat. The cell smelled of strong disinfect mingled with a faint odour of urine. She wondered how long she would have to remain banged up for. All she had was a narrow bed with a stained mattress and a silver toilet, minus the seat, screwed into the wall. It was spartan to say the least.

When the door thudded behind her and she heard the clank of the key turning in the lock, Stephanie sat down in the corner of the police cell hugging her legs closely to her chest. What a wonderful way to spend Christmas day. She imagined people up and down the country laughing and joking, enjoying their Christmas lunches, pulling crackers and wearing daft hats. She wished she was anywhere except where she was right now.

A thought had been niggling away at her ever since she had been brought to Pontcae Police Station—what if she really had killed Lawrence? Could someone die from overdosing on laxative powder? No doubt they could if they were given an extremely large quantity, but she had only given him two or three times the normal dosage. The intention had only been to give him enough to put him out of action for a few hours so she could escape from the cruiser, out of his clutches. In any case, who knows what might have happened to her if she had stayed a prisoner on that boat? He had already raped her the once, so that would be a huge possibility. Maybe he would have beaten her up as well, or even...

Someone slid back a small door on top of the cell, "I've brought you some lunch," said a middle-aged detention officer with a cheerful attitude. It was Christmas for the police as well and they were only doing their jobs.

She heard him unlock the door and he handed her a plastic tray with portions for meat and vegetables, plastic cutlery and a cup of tea. "Thanks," she whispered as she took the tray from him.

"Now if you eat all that up, I'll fetch you some pudding as well." He winked. Any other occasion and she would have laughed, but this was serious. Being accused of murdering someone. She wondered how Lawrence had died. He had many enemies that was for sure.

Stephanie managed a few mouthfuls of the cardboard tasting food and drank the tea. At least the tea tasted normal. In the distance, she heard the sound of people laughing and joking. Probably the custody sergeant and the man who had brought her meal. They'd probably have preferred to be somewhere else today, too.

She lay down on the mattress, not caring that it was dirty any more and drifted off to sleep. The next thing she knew, the door opened and a man dressed in a navy pinstripe suit, holding a brief case, stood staring at her.

Stephanie rubbed her eyes. For a moment, she had forgotten where she was. "Who are you?"

"Don't worry, I'm here to help you. I've been employed by Mr Pryce-Jones. I'm Warren Parker, your solicitor." He extended his hand in a firm grip. She liked that. It showed he was someone with strength of character.

"Am I glad to see you." She smiled.

"They've arranged for us to use an interview room across the way. We may not have much time, though, before the police want to interview you themselves."

****

Dylan was pleased that he had managed to contact Warren Parker, although he felt a little guilty at having to bother Matt. Matt had enough on his plate now with the imminent arrival of his baby and the complications of Sandy's pregnancy.

Dylan rang the police station and asked if he could see Stephanie, but was told he couldn't. If she was allowed out on bail, they would inform him.

There was nothing else for it; he had to keep himself busy. For now there was nothing he could do but wait. He went along to the Camelot room to check on the wedding party, pleased to see that it was all going well by the look on the bride and groom's faces. He was glad that Steph had stepped in to help reconcile the couple. When he had satisfied himself that all was running smoothly, he popped over to Jim at the bar and asked him to send a couple of magnums of champagne to the wedding party with his compliments.

Now all he had to do was find his parents and explain the situation with Stephanie to them.

****

Stephanie sat on the opposite site of the table to Warren Parker. He had a serious kind of face, she mused. He looked to be in his mid fifties with greying hair at the temples. He lifted his expensive-looking, leather brief case onto the table and pulled out a notepad and pen. She noticed he had two gold rings on his fingers: one, a thick wedding band, the other, some kind of a Celtic knot with a small diamond inset. Maybe he could afford such luxuries with the fees he charged. How on earth was she expected to pay for his services? As if he could read her mind, he put down the paper and pen and said, "Don't worry, the fees are all taken care of by Mr Pryce-Jones."

She nodded, but inwardly cringed at the though of compromising her independence by indebting herself to someone else, especially after the way Lawrence had emotionally blackmailed her, but then, Dylan was hardly another Black, was he?

"Now, down to business," Warren announced, "did you murder Lawrence Black?"

His direct form of questioning totally took her aback.

"No, certainly not!" she cried indignantly.

Then he surprised her by saying, "Good! That's exactly what I wanted you to say."

"You do believe me, don't you?"

"My dear, it matters not a jot whether I believe you or not, it's whether a jury would believe you if this were to go to court."

Stephanie swallowed hard. Why on earth should she have to go to court? She hadn't done anything. "By the way, how did he die?" She held her breath, hoping upon hope that he wasn't going to inform her that it was by poisoning.

"He was shot—in the back of the head at close range. That's all the police have told me so far."

She let out a long breath. So it was definitely nothing to do with her. But who? How? Another thought struck her. If she hadn't run out on him, maybe he wouldn't have been shot. *And if you hadn't got away, you might have been killed too,* her inner voice told her.

"Tell me, Miss Baynham…is there something you wish to tell me?"

So, he had an idea that she was worried about something? She had to give him credit, he seemed like the type of man who worked very much by his instincts.

"Only that I was with him last night. He kidnapped me and took me to the quayside and locked me in his boat. I was petrified. You see, we used to live together and it was not unusual for me to suffer at his hands."

"By suffer you mean he hit you?"

"Yes. He also raped me once."

Warren Parker was expressionless as he jotted down the details.

"So, is it fair to say you were frightened of him?"

"Oh, totally. I mean, last night he threatened to take me with him. He was leaving the country for Ireland. So I tried to find something on the boat to knock him out to allow myself time to escape. Only, I couldn't find any tranquillisers or sleeping tablets, but I did manage to find some laxative powder which I put in his coffee."

"So what happened then?"

"After a while, he tried to get me in his bedroom. I was afraid to refuse and hoped upon hope that the powder would work before anything happened and thankfully, it did, just in time. He was doubled up in agony and left me to go to the bathroom. In the meantime, I managed to get out of the boat." She felt her heart pounding as she related the tale.

"And what happened next?"

"I got back to my apartment, it's only minutes away. Tried to get a taxi, but in the end, had to ring an old friend, Matt Walker. Unfortunately, I saw a car drawing up outside like his—it was the same model. I foolishly assumed it was him and walked over to the car, only to discover it was Danny King, one of Lawrence's henchmen."

"What happened then?"

"He managed to get me inside the car and drove into Cardiff. I got him to drop me outside a hotel to make out I was staying there, so that he wouldn't know I was staying at the castle. I managed to get back to the castle pretty late, and today, I was shocked when the police arrested me."

"I see. So what time would you say it was when you got to the boat?"

"When I was kidnapped by Lawrence you mean?"

Warren Parker nodded.

"I would say around six p.m. Yes, that's about right. I remember glancing at a clock he had in the shape of a ship's wheel on the wall. I think it said five past six."

"And what time was it when you escaped from the boat?"

"I don't know for sure, I would guess it was around two and a half hours later..."

He scribbled down the information. "I need you to think carefully about those times."

"Well, it was definitely past five-thirty when I left Matt and Sandy's place. I wanted to get back to the castle. I was due to work there at seven p.m. I needed time to get myself ready. I know it was gone eight o'clock as when I got back to my apartment, there was a Christmas movie just starting."

"That might help a little. If you can remember the name of it, we can search the television listings to verify the time."

"What happens now?"

"As I said, you'll be interviewed by the police shortly. They'll tape every word you say, but don't worry—I'll be present. We should also know shortly the results of a post mortem on Black."

Stephanie gulped, Lawrence was dead and less than twenty four hours ago she had almost been in his bed.

****

Dylan found his parents snoozing in the lounge in front of the television, Mimi curled up on his mother's lap. He bent down to switch it off. They looked like a pair of naughty children. He was just about to leave when his father gave a loud snort, opening his eyes.

"What's happening? Has Christmas been and gone?" he muttered.

"No, Dad. It's only early evening."

"So I haven't missed my Christmas dinner then, have I?" He chuckled, rubbing his stomach. "I don't know about your mother, but I'm famished. What time are we eating?"

"I'm sorry, Dad. We'll have to postpone it for now."

"Something wrong is there, son? Is the chef playing up again?"

"No, it's nothing like that. Come over here, I don't want to alarm Mother."

Reginald followed Dylan outside into the corridor.

"So what is it then?"

"It's Stephanie...she's been arrested for the murder of Lawrence Black."

"But that's preposterous! How can that be? Last night we were looking for her because we feared what he might do to her."

"I know," whispered Dylan for fear his mother should hear. "I don't know exactly what's happened, but it sure has nothing to do with Steph."

Dylan heard his mother moving around, fussing over her little dog and getting up out of her chair, switching the television back on. He heard the familiar tune for the regional news being played.

It was too late. The presenter announced: "Local business man, Lawrence Black was found dead in his cruiser this morning. Residents at Cardiff Bay reported hearing a gun shot in the early hours of the morning. A woman is being questioned at Pontcae Police Station." Then the picture switched from the presenter to a local reporter standing outside the boat, a picture of Lawrence and another of one his clubs. Back to the presenter.

"Police would like to hear from anyone who was in the vicinity yesterday evening from the time of six p.m onwards. A special phone line has been set up at Pontcae Police Station." The phone number flashed on the screen along with a picture of Detective Sergeant Hunter.

****

Stephanie sat in the police interview room alongside Warren Parker, D.S. Hunter and D.C. Miller sat opposite.

Hunter slipped a cassette into the tape recorder and said, "This interview is being tape recorded and it may be given in evidence if your case is brought to trial. At the conclusion, you will be provided with a copy of the tape and a form explaining what will happen to the tapes. We are in an interview room at Pontcae Police Station. The time is seventeen-hundred hours."

"I am Detective Sergeant Dawn Hunter, the other officer present is Detective Constable Richard Miller. I am interviewing, 'Please state your full name and date of birth'."

"Stephanie Baynham 15th of May 1979."

"Also present is Miss Baynham's solicitor, Warren Parker..." she continued, "Miss Baynham, is there any reason why you should not be interviewed at this time?"

"I'm sorry I don't understand what you mean?"

"Are you under the influence of drink, drugs, or any medication that could affect you at this present time?"

Stephanie shook her head.

"I'm afraid you have to answer yes or no as the tape is recording," Hunter said sternly.

"Sorry. No. I haven't had any alcohol today, I don't take drugs and I'm not on any medication."

"Good. You do not have to say anything but it may harm your defence if you do not mention when questioned, something which you later rely on in court. Anything you do say may be given in evidence. Do you understand?"

"Yes."

"What do you think I meant by that, Miss Baynham?"

Stephanie swallowed, "That I don't have to speak if I don't want to, but if I do not speak it may harm my defence. If I do answer your questions, anything I say may be used as evidence in court."

"Right. Mr Parker, the following is the information disclosed to you prior to the interview. Will you confirm that this was the information disclosed, that you have had sufficient time to consult with your client and your role in this interview?"

Warren Parker sounded cool as he replied, "Yes."

The policewoman continued, "The reason for this interview is because you have been arrested for the offence of the murder of Lawrence Black and I am going to question you about this matter. This is your opportunity to provide an explanation. During the interview, I and my colleague will be asking you questions that we consider are relevant to the enquiry, and we will be making notes. If you wish to reply, please answer clearly. Do you understand me?"

Stephanie cleared her throat. "Yes."

"In the early hours of December the 25th at around 2.15 am, the body of a man, who we believe to be Lawrence Black, was found on a boat named the 'Seafarer' at the marina at Cardiff Bay. From an initial examination, it appears that this person was shot in the back of the head. Evidence was found at the scene which suggests that he had earlier been in the company of another person or persons. Since that time, we have received an anonymous phone call to say that you were the last person to see him alive and you were on the boat with him for some time the evening before. What have you to say on this matter?"

Stephanie glanced across at Warren Parker who appeared as if about to say something, but instead nodded at her to answer the question.

"Yes, I was in his company but…"

"So you were alone with Lawrence Black on the 24th of December?"

"Yes. I was."

"Between what times?"

"From about five-thirty when he forced me into his car. We arrived at his cruiser at around 6:05 p.m. and I left about two and a half hours later."

"When you were on the cruiser with Mr Black, what did you do?"

"Well, I didn't want to be there in the first place. I

mean, he had kidnapped me, so I had to think of a way of getting out. He said he was going to leave the country for Ireland and he was going to take me with him."

"So, there was no way you wanted to go with him. Why?"

"Because I used to be involved with him. I was his girlfriend until about two years ago. I also worked for him. I didn't like his seedy activities."

"So how long were you involved with him for?"

"Around eighteen months."

D.C. Miller butted in, "That was a long time to be involved with someone if you didn't like what they were doing, isn't it?"

Stephanie cleared her throat again. "Yes, I know it was very foolish of me. But he had a kind of hold over me."

"A hold?" D.C. Miller persisted.

"Yes. Emotional blackmail, that kind of thing. Plus, he wasn't averse to giving me the odd slap or two."

"So what made you finally walk away from the relationship?"

"It was when he employed me at the club. I got the impression he wanted me to give extras."

"Extras?" Miller shot her a sly smile.

Stephanie felt her face grow hot. She wondered if the policeman was getting a kick out of asking her such questions. "You know, he wanted me to provide sexual favours for clients, that kind of thing."

"I see. So would you say he was trying to get you into prostitution?"

Stephanie let out a long breath. "Yes. After that, I knew he couldn't really have loved me, so I left him."

Miller raked his fingers through his gelled back hair. "So back to last night on the boat. You say you left him two and a half hours later. How did you manage to get away?"

What could she say that wouldn't incriminate her? "I managed to get hold of the key and made a dash for it."

"That all sounds a little too easy. Surely a big strapping man like Lawrence Black could have caught you?"

She could feel her heart beat quickening. "All right.

I'll tell you…"

"You don't have to say anymore if you don't want to Miss Baynam," Warren Parker intervened.

"No. I think I need to tell them the truth."

Chapter Nine

"Is Stephanie the person the police are holding to question regarding this Lawrence Black's death?" Daphne asked Dylan, looking a lot more composed than when he had seen her on the cooking sherry earlier in the kitchen.

"Yes, I'm afraid she is. Mother, I can tell you categorically that she didn't do it."

"I never doubted that for a second, Dylan. But why is she tied up in all of this? I don't understand."

"She was involved with Black a couple of years ago. She's absolutely petrified of him. He kidnapped her last night and, as you could see for yourself, she managed to get away. Unfortunately, the police say that someone tipped them off anonymously to say that she was the last person to see Lawrence alive. And as he took her to his boat, there's plenty of forensic evidence to support this."

"But we can't just stay here and do nothing. We have to do what we can to help the poor girl."

"Don't you think I've thought of that? The police have told me that, for now, there is nothing I can do but wait."

"What about going back to the club and making a few more enquiries?" Reg interrupted.

"I don't think that would be a good idea. It might be dangerous," Dylan said. "I do have another idea, though. You and I, Father, are going on a little outing."

****

"What was it you wanted to say, Miss Baynham?" D.S. Hunter probed.

Stephanie looked at Warren Parker for a moment. "Are you sure about this?" he whispered. She nodded.

"Last night, when Lawrence kidnapped me, I was so frightened..."

"Frightened in what sort of a way?"

"In case he hurt me. Anyhow, I knew there was no way he was going to let me walk out of the boat, so I figured the best thing would be to put him out of action."

"Put him out of action?"

"Well, I mean there was no way I could overpower a big man like him, so I thought I'd try to drug him."

Both police officers looked at one another. Oh dear, maybe she had said the wrong thing. She continued, "I was looking for something that might put him to sleep for a short while, like sleeping tablets or tranquillizers. I couldn't find any as his medicine cabinet in the bathroom was locked, but I did come across some laxative powder in the kitchen. I managed to slip some into his coffee without him knowing."

"What effect did that have?" she persisted.

"Nothing much at first, so I had to give him some more. Eventually, he got me in the bedroom..."

D.C. Miller interrupted, "Was this voluntary or against your will?"

"I went willingly, hoping that the powder would do its trick before too long."

"You say you went willingly, yet you claim to have been afraid of this man?"

"I know it sounds strange, but I had to make it look as if I was going along with what he wanted. Eventually, he doubled up in pain and went to the bathroom. The laxative was beginning to work."

D.S. Hunter shot Miller a scathing glance as she took back over the line of enquiry. "What happened next, Miss Baynham?"

"I managed to find the key to get out of the boat and escaped. I ran back to my apartment."

"What time was this?"

"It would have been around eight-thirty. There was a film on the television that was just starting. I remember what it was now..." Stephanie said, looking at Warren.

"What was it?"

"Scrooge."

"You mean the colour musical version?"

"No, an old black and white version starring Alistair Sim."

"Right. We can check that out for timing of course,

but it doesn't mean to say that you saw it at that time. You could have read it in the T.V listings."

"Well that's where you're wrong," Stephanie said, starting to feel like she wanted to slap her across the face. Didn't the woman believe her? "The television announcer said there was a change to the schedule and it appears that the film went out at the last minute."

D.C. Miller nodded at his partner as if to confirm that this was correct.

"That concludes the interview for now. Is there anything you wish to add or clarify in connection with what you have said?"

"Just that I didn't intend any harm to come to Lawrence Black. I just wanted to escape from the boat."

Dawn Hunter nodded and repeated, "That concludes the interview, the time is now seventeen hundred-forty-five hours and I am stopping the recording."

Stephanie let out a long sigh and relaxed in her chair. "That wasn't so bad," she whispered to Warren Parker.

"You think it's over?" he asked incredulously, "We're only stopping for a break."

Stephanie slid down in her chair. When was this day going to end?

****

"So, what did you have in mind?" Reg asked Dylan as they drove out of the castle grounds in the direction of Cardiff.

"I thought we'd pay a little visit to Lawrence's other club, 'Night Zone'," Dylan replied, muttering under his breath as a car pulled out in front of them, the driver failing to use indicators.

"But what's the purpose of that? You've already said it might be too dangerous."

"Look, I have to do something. I feel so helpless. It's the only thing I can think of, Dad. If it makes you feel better, you can wait in the car and send for the police if I don't come back out."

"No. Definitely not," His father said forcefully. "I won't let you go into the club on your own. But shouldn't you be leaving everything to the police anyhow?"

"For now, all I can think about is Stephanie scared

out of her wits being interviewed by them. You know, when I first met her, people warned me about her, saying she was trouble. A meddler, a minx, a vamp, they called her. Yet, underneath that façade, I saw something in her that others couldn't see."

"And what did you see in her, Dylan?"

Dylan swallowed the lump in his throat. "All I saw was this vulnerable little girl who needed to be loved."

"She's really got under your skin, hasn't she?" Reg gently patted Dylan's shoulder.

Dylan didn't reply. He just kept his eyes on the road ahead.

****

"Tell me, Miss Baynham, do you normally wear perfume?" Hunter asked as the questioning resumed.

What did they want to know that for?

Stephanie nodded, then remembering the interview was being taped, answered, "Yes."

"So what brand of perfume do you use?"

"Opium, by Yves St Laurent."

"I see. And were you wearing Opium last night when you were in Lawrence Black's company."

"Yes, I believe I was."

"What about lipstick?"

"Lipstick?"

"Were you wearing any last night?"

"Yes."

"What colour was it?"

"Iced Pink. I can show you the exact lipstick—I handed my bag over when I was searched—my make up bag is inside. Why do you want to know?"

"Forensics."

"Yes, but I've already explained to you, I was on the boat with Lawrence, I did make coffee and so, consequently, I would have left lipstick marks on my coffee cup."

"It seems, Miss Baynham, that Mr Black had another female visitor last night."

"So, I'm off the hook then?" Stephanie said, sitting up and feeling more hopeful.

"Why would you believe you were off the hook? In our eyes there is still the possibility that you murdered Black.

It's up to you to prove otherwise." The policewoman sat back in her chair. She had a habit, Stephanie noted, of hitting the nail on the head.

The interview was going worse than she thought. Surely, whoever else was on the boat with Black must have murdered him? Maybe it was Lucy Clarke? She'd had a bit of a thing for Black. She must have loved it when Stephanie had disappeared for all that length of time.

D.S. Hunter spoke slowly and deliberately. "I put it to you, Miss Baynham, that you were so afraid of Black and what he might do to you that you took the opportunity to kill him last night?"

"No, I didn't do it!" Stephanie got to her feet. Warren Parker took her arm and guided her back into her seat.

"Keep calm," he whispered in her ear.

"What were you doing last month?" Hunter persisted with her tough methods of questioning as D.C. Miller sat back in his chair with a smirk on his face.

"I was out of the country."

"Where were you?"

"I've been staying in Milan for the past nine months with my grandparents."

D.S. Hunter's face fell. What was the matter with the woman? Did she want to pin the case at her feet? "I'll need verification," she said sharply.

"I can easily give you that. I worked at a local family run hotel most of the time I was there. Mr Viazzani, the owner, can vouch for me."

"Write the number down here," commanded D.C. Miller, handing her a pen and paper.

"So," Hunter said, regaining her composure, "what made you go to Milan in the first place?"

"I wanted to get away from him, Black."

"That seems a little drastic, leaving the country."

"Believe me, I would have done anything to have got him off my back." She bit her lip in an attempt to hold back the tears. Had she said the wrong thing again? She looked at Warren Parker who raised a silver eyebrow. What must that have sounded like?

Like she wanted to kill Lawrence, that's what.

Chapter Ten

'Night Zone' was all in darkness when Dylan and his father drew up outside. Of course, he should have thought, it was Christmas day. Not that many places opened on the actual day itself. He got out of the car and scouted around the building. The street was quiet, except for two young women who were singing at the tops of their inebriated voices in the distance.

"Come on, Dylan," Reg shouted from the car, "you might as well give up and go back home. The club is shut."

Dylan ignored his father and carried on looking through the windows. He crouched down and peered through a letter box in a side door.

"There's a light on in one of the rooms," he whispered to his father when he got back to the car. "I think I'll try knocking."

"Wouldn't that be foolish? I mean…what are you going to say? 'By the way I know one of you killed Lawrence Black, now tell the police so I can get my girlfriend safely back home?'" Put that way, it sounded ridiculous.

For a moment, Dylan considered leaving things as they were, but a vision of Stephanie sitting sad and desolate at the police station took over and fired him on for a show down.

He walked forcefully back up the steps and rang a bell. When no one came to answer, he hammered on the door with his fists. Eventually, the door opened slowly, and he was allowed to see the foyer, his father following closely behind him.

"What do you want?" growled a tall, thick set man in a black suit.

"I'd like to talk with Danny King, please?"

The man looked Dylan up and down. "What's the nature of your business?" Did this man think he was a drug dealer, the police, or what?

"It's a personal matter. I'm sorry, I can't tell you."

The man started to close the door but Dylan inserted his foot in the way. The door continued to close and Dylan was about to yell out in pain, when it was released and the man said, "You'd better come this way."

Both men followed him along a dimly lit corridor and down a set of stairs. Finally, they came face to face with a small group of men who were in the middle of a card game.

"Here Bob," the man shouted. "These guys want to talk with Mr King."

All the men except for one looked up and laughed, the other carried on looking at his cards. Then he took out a card, flipped it on the table and looked up at Dylan and his father standing at the bottom of the wrought iron staircase. He appeared to be a cool customer.

"I'm Danny King. What do you want me for?" He asked with a sullen expression.

"Is there somewhere we could talk in private?" Dylan swallowed.

"You want somewhere private?" Dylan nodded at him. "I'll give you private. Get out of here." For a moment, Dylan thought he was addressing him and his father, but the men got up from the table and pushed past them on the stairway.

"Thanks," Dylan said.

"Don't thank me yet. Sit down." Dylan and Reg sat opposite him across the card strewn table.

"Now, what do you men want?"

****

Stephanie was beginning to feel weary. She was tired of all the questioning and had managed to rest in the cell for about an hour when she heard the door unlocking and Warren Parker stepped in.

"We're going back to the interview room again," he said with a smile.

"Oh no. I can't take much more of this." She felt like putting her head in her hands and sobbing her heart out.

How could one day start on a high with a wedding and end with imprisonment in a police cell? It was all getting a bit too much.

"Don't worry." His voice was soothing. "You're not being interviewed, I have some good news for you."

He led her down the corridor and an officer let them into the interview room.

"Sit down," Parker said, "the results of the post mortem are back. You'll be relieved to hear that there are no significant traces of laxative in the deceased's body. What I mean is, yes, sure they could find a trace of it, but not much more than a person would take if they were constipated. So whatever you did, you didn't kill him."

She let out a long breath. At least she wasn't the person who was responsible for his death—that was a relief. "I'm so glad to hear that," she said as she sat back in her chair. "What now?"

"The cause of death, of course, is the gunshot wound to the head and to be honest with you, I don't think the police will be able to hold you for much longer. The only evidence they have is you were on his boat last night. They'd need more evidence to keep you here. I think all being well, they might release you on police bail shortly."

****

Dylan wrung his hands and cleared his throat. This wasn't going to be easy. What was he going to say that wouldn't endanger Stephanie and wouldn't make himself sound like a plonker?

"It's like this...My friend is being held as a murder suspect at Pontcae Police Station and I think you might be able to help me."

"Me? What on earth is this to do with me?"

"Well, I know that Stephanie Baynham didn't murder Lawrence, and I know that you gave her a lift into Cardiff after she left the boat. Would you be willing to tell the police that?"

"And what's in it for me?" King stood, his hands balled into fists, glaring at Dylan. His face now reddened and a twitch appearing in his left eye

"I just thought you might have done it as a favour," Dylan said, glancing at his father.

"A favour!" King banged his fist on the table and laid

back his head in mock laughter. "Tell me, Sunshine, what sort of a favour do I owe you?"

Dylan cleared his throat. "I happen to know something about you, Mr King. Something you wouldn't like the police to know."

Danny King leaned forward again and grabbed Dylan by the lapels of his jacket. "What do you mean you know something about me? Are you threatening me?" he growled.

Dylan feared he may have gone too far. "Look, I'm just appealing to your good nature, Mr King..."

"Let's get this straight. You have something on me that you'll probably go to the police with if I don't let the police know I gave Stephanie a lift last night?"

"Yes. That's it in a nutshell." Dylan hoped King wouldn't notice the faint tremor in his voice. Right now, he would rather have been elsewhere—but he knew he had to do this for Steph.

"And how do you know that I haven't already spoken to the police? You don't, do you?"

Dylan swallowed. "Err, no, I don't."

"Then don't come around to my club making idle threats when you don't know the half of it."

Dylan noticed King now referred to the club as his. Maybe an arrangement had been made if anything happened to Lawrence Black that he would take over. What a good motive to kill Black.

"I think it's better if we go," whispered Reg. Maybe his father was right. He was an old man and he could do without all this drama.

"Yes, I think it's better if you do. I'll just get my men to show you to the door," King said, picking up a telephone. "Andy, show these men out—the back door, if you will." King's voice had more than a threat of menace to it. Dylan was beginning to regret coming at all.

Two of the men who had earlier been sitting around the table playing cards, rushed down the stairs and quickly escorted Dylan and his father up the wrought iron staircase. The thugs dragged them roughly, banging their shins against the steps as they forced them along. Dylan breathed a sigh of relief as they were shown the back door. "That was a close call," he said to his father and he bent over to rub his legs. Before Reg had a chance to answer, three men jumped out from behind some large bins and started laying into them, fists flying.

Dylan tried to avoid their punches but one of them caught him with a left hook to his cheek and he rebounded against a brick wall, hitting his head. The pair were relentless, no sooner had Dylan drawn a breath than one of them was hitting him again. Dylan heard his father call out.

"Don't hurt my father," Dylan yelled. "You have an advantage. Two against one. He's more than your ages put together."

"Leave Granddad alone!" one of the men commanded and two of them held Dylan against the wall, whilst the third punched him in the stomach. Reg tried his best to prise them off, but they took it in turns. Dylan gasped, winded at each punch wondering if they would ever stop. He was starting to feel he might lose consciousness but at the back of his mind was the thought, if they were all hitting him they were leaving his father alone.

The man who wore a thick, gold ring was the worse of the three, as Dylan felt the metal gauge into the skin on his face, the bastard grinned. He felt the excruciating agony as it pierced his cheek and something wet and warm trickled down his face. It was a few seconds before he realised it was his own blood. The pain made him want to break down and cry, but no way was he going to show any sign of weakness in front of them or his father. They were relentless until the back door opened and Andy said, "King says to leave it be now. He's been watching you on the security camera. He doesn't want you to kill the bloke, just rough him up a little."

The three men started back in the direction of the club but one returned to where Dylan was lying and kicked him in the face.

"You savage bastards!" Reg shouted.

"Don't, Dad," Dylan groaned, holding his head. Whatever happened, this was his mess and no way did he want his father getting hurt.

Reg knelt down at Dylan's side. "I'm going to help you up now, son." He said softly, "then we're going to walk to the car and I'm going to run you to the hospital."

"No...no...hospital," Dylan groaned. He feared they might keep him in, he wouldn't be any help to Stephanie then. "I shouldn't have come here, Dad. Just take me home."

"Okay." Dylan could have sworn he heard his father choke back a sob. He was still alive. That's all that mattered for now. He had made it out of the club alive and he was glad he hadn't told King that he had heard him confess to Jenni's murder.

****

Warren Parker had been correct in his assumptions. The custody sergeant told Stephanie she would be allowed out on one month's police bail. But she had been disappointed she hadn't been able to contact Dylan. She had spoken to Daphne, who had insisted on coming down in a taxi to fetch her.

"Are you all right?" Daphne asked, as Stephanie climbed into the cab next to her.

Stephanie started to sob and Daphne put her arm around her. "It's been quite an ordeal for you, hasn't it? Don't be afraid to let it out. We'll be home shortly." Stephanie was surprised how motherly Daphne was being towards her. If she listened to Dylan, he had her believing that Daphne was the mother from hell.

The ride home past the Christmas lights was quite comforting, knowing she was free, even if it was only for one month. What puzzled her was the fact Dylan couldn't be contacted. He had promised he would be there for her.

Daphne paid the cab driver, draping a comforting arm around Stephanie as they walked into the castle. "I'll just go pour us a brandy each," Daphne said soothingly. Stephanie nodded and smiled.

She sat in the lounge area, waiting for Daphne to return with the welcome drink. Startled, she jumped when she heard someone call from outside. It sounded like Reg's voice. What was going on? Jim was already on his way out and she followed after him.

She watched as Reg and Jim lifted Dylan from the back seat. He was stretched flat out. She wondered for a moment if he was drunk, until she saw the state of him. He had cuts to his forehead and chin and a black eye, blood dripped slowly from his nose.

"Dylan, what's happened?" she shouted.

Dylan managed to open one eye as Jim and Reg walked him into the castle. "I'll explain later. I'm so glad you're out, Steph. Dad, walk me around the side of the castle, I'll get to my quarters that way. I don't want the guests to see me like this." He let out a groan and collapsed in a heap on the floor.

"Jim, phone for an ambulance," Stephanie commanded.

"No." Reg put his hand firmly on her shoulder. "Dylan doesn't want that. We'll carry him inside and phone for his family doctor."

Steph nodded. She didn't mind as long as he was getting medical attention. She loved him so much it hurt to see him in this state. A moment ago, everything looked great—she was a free woman—even if it was only temporary. But now, she couldn't make out what had happened. She needed an answer.

Chapter Eleven

Dylan winced as Stephanie cleansed his wounds with cotton wool balls and antiseptic solution.

"Look Dylan," she advised as she carried on dabbing at the raw cuts. "You're going to have to take on board what Doctor Quinlan said, you need plenty of rest for a few days..."

"But how can I rest?" He let out a long groan. "It's a busy time of year for me."

"Let me worry about that. You tell me what you want doing and I'll get it done for you."

He stretched out his hand and took hers, making her palm tingle with electricity. It was still there, that attraction she had for him had never gone away. He reached out, gently stroking her cheek. How could she leave him? She had planned on getting away in the New Year but she couldn't abandon him now.

"You're so good to me, do you know that?"

She smiled and carried on cleaning his wounds. "Don't forget, the doctor suggested you get an x-ray to be on the safe side." He nodded. "Now come on, tell me, how did you end up looking like a raw piece of meat?"

"I asked the wrong questions..." He let out a hallow laugh and then clutched at his ribs. It obviously hurt him to even do that.

"What sort of questions?" She wasn't going to let him off the hook that easily.

"Dad and I went to 'Night Zone' to find Danny King. I wanted him to tell the police he gave you a lift on Christmas Eve. I made the mistake of telling him I had something on him."

"And do you?"

Dylan nodded. "I heard him confess with his own lips

117

that he had killed Jenni."

Stephanie's heart started beating wildly. King wasn't a man to mess with. In some respects, he was more dangerous than Black was. "So he got some of his thugs to lay into you, I bet?"

"'Fraid so. Don't worry. I won't be going back again anytime soon."

"Dylan, you don't realise the seedy world you are getting into. This isn't Eastenders, you know. Why do you think I got out? In any case, you were wasting your time."

He quirked an eyebrow.

"King has already been questioned by the police and confirmed that he gave me a lift."

Dylan closed his eyes for a moment and let out a long groan of frustration. Then said, "Do you think he killed Lawrence?"

She chewed her bottom lip. "I really don't know. I mean, there was no love lost between the two of them. That was common knowledge. One thing I have found out though, is that there was another woman on the boat yesterday."

"Another woman? That's interesting. Who do you imagine that was?"

"Well, unless Jenni has somehow come back to life…then it could have been…no, it couldn't, could it?"

"Who?"

"Lucy Clarke. The girl I saw in the department store when I went shopping. She had the hots for Black. When I left, I think she tried to step into my shoes."

Dylan winced as she dabbed on the last of the antiseptic. "I think we have got to find her," he said.

****

Stephanie arose bright and early on Boxing Day morning. There was no time for a lie in anymore—she had work to do. And that work was helping Dylan to run the hotel. After a quick cup of coffee and a shower, she went in search of Chef to see how he was managing in the kitchen. Everything appeared to be in control, so she went to check on the domestic staff. The wedding party would be booking out today, so all would quieten down shortly. On the way back, she called into Dylan's quarters and found Daphne there tending her son.

"Can you talk some sense into this boy of mine?" Daphne said, her eyes pleading with Stephanie.

"What's the matter?" Stephanie could see Dylan looked a bit irritated with his mother.

"I can't get him to eat anything. I brought him a breakfast tray and he's just sitting there refusing to make any conversation."

Stephanie put her arm around the woman's shoulder and whispered, "You go and get your own breakfast, I'll see to Dylan."

Daphne smiled, bent over the bed to kiss her son and quietly left the room.

"So, Mr-I'm-acting-like-a-little-boy, when are you going to grow up?" Stephanie whipped the bedclothes from him.

"Hey! Give me those back!"

She sat down on the bed next to him and held his hand. It looked bruised and swollen. "You really should get an x-ray, you know."

"I know." He gazed into her eyes and brushed away a lock of her hair that had fallen over her face. "Thanks for caring. I have been acting like a little boy as far as my mother's concerned, I know. And if I'm honest with myself, I wanted her to fuss over me. I never had that when I was a child."

"Yes, but you're a grown man now. Get up and have a shower. I'll bring you some fresh coffee and cook you something while you're getting ready, then I'm taking you to the hospital for an x-ray."

"Yes, ma'am!" He gave a mock salute and stood by the side of the bed. Then he locked eyes with hers and said, "So, the police have granted you a month's bail. At least I'll have you for that length of time."

"Don't joke, Dylan, please," she knew her voice had a catch to it and if she thought about things too much, she might just break down and cry. She had accused Dylan of acting like a child just now, but deep down she knew he was all man. Man enough to face the likes of Danny King. Man enough to even risk his life for her.

"Sorry," he said as he lightly touched her arm. A surge of electricity travelled the length of her arm, almost robbing her of her breath. "You know I care about you, don't you?" She nodded and made for the door before he could see what sort of an effect he had on her.

"I'll be back with a fresh breakfast for you shortly." She took a deep breath to compose herself and closed the door, fanning her face. Either the central heating was turned up way too high or her internal boiler was skyrocketing through the roof.

The kitchen was empty for once, everything cleared away. All the guests had probably eaten their breakfast by now and Chef must have been taking a well earned break. She got what she needed from the large refrigerator, turned on the hob and fried some bacon rashers.

Cracking open two eggs, she dropped them into the frying pan alongside the rashers and watched them splatter and sizzle away. What was this emotion she was feeling right now? Her heart felt heavy. Guilt, probably. Guilt for coming back to Wales and involving Dylan in her little mess. She should have stayed in Milan—but it would have been difficult. Her grandparents were due to move into a smaller apartment in the New Year and she had felt it was time to come back home. But what for? *Dylan, of course*, her inner voice reminded her.

What had she been expecting when she got back? Hearts and flowers? For Lawrence to have magically disappeared? Yet, now he was dead, she didn't feel any happier.

As she watched the eggs frying, she wondered about Matt and Sandy. Had the baby been born yet? She made up her mind to get in touch with them after she had taken Dylan to the hospital.

****

Dylan winced as the hot jets of water sprayed against his battered and bruised body. This was pain like no other as the water seeped into his wounds. He should have taken the painkillers his doctor had prescribed with his breakfast. It served him right, he supposed. How on earth could Stephanie have involved herself in such a seedy world? There were plenty of Kings and Blacks in the outside world, but this was the first time he had ever had an encounter with any of them. Money and power was what they craved and they stamped over anyone in their path to get to them. Even killing to do so.

He planned to work on some of his fashion designs over the Christmas break. The New Year brought new shows and new ideas. He'd even toyed with asking Stephanie to model for him. His heart pounded, blood coursing through his veins as he imagined her wearing one of his designs. He'd been working on a luxury underwear design for the Bridal Collection, using only the purest silks and satins. In his mind, it was just as important what the bride wore beneath her dress. To look good on her big day, she had to feel good too.

Imagining Stephanie wearing the champagne Thai silk slip, matching panties and stockings made him give a little groan. The woman was sex on legs, but she was more than that. People saw her as a vamp, but she was intelligent too and she had a caring side. He had been a witness to that on more than one occasion.

Yes, to have one more time with Stephanie wearing that little outfit, in his bedroom, would make him one happy man.

****

Stephanie drove the car through Pontcae towards the direction of the hospital. As she glanced across at the sea, she marvelled at how fierce the waves were, as high rollers crashed upon the beach. No one could master the sea. It was its own master. "Fancy a walk on the beach later, when we return from the hospital?" she asked Dylan.

"As long as they don't keep me in," he joked.

"Trust me, they won't. They try to get everyone, the walking wounded included, home for the Christmas holidays if they can."

"How do you know that?"

"I used to be a nurse."

"I didn't know that." he said, sounding bemused.

"Well, you do now." She changed gear and turned into a small lane that led to a larger road and finally they pulled up outside Pontcae General Hospital.

"Thanks." He leaned over and gave her a peck on the cheek. "I don't know what I'd do without you."

Was it only a few short days ago when they had driven almost in silence from the airport to Wales? It was unbelievable so much had happened since then. It was almost like Christmas had never happened at all.

As if reading her mind, he looked at her and said, "You know, we didn't have much of a Christmas, did we?"

"I know, I'm sorry about that." She bit her lip.

"Hey, don't get me wrong. I wasn't blaming you or anything. It's just that I think we should celebrate it again."

"How do you mean?"

"I'm going to ask Chef if he will prepare a special meal for you and me tonight. He won't have so much work once the wedding party has left"

"That's a nice idea. But what about Reg and Daphne?"

"Yes, we'll invite them too if you like."

"I do like."

She easily found a parking space, got out of the car and he followed her into the casualty department, hoping he wouldn't have to stay too long.

****

As they strolled along the sands, deep in thought, taking in the sounds of the sea, Dylan said, "I think we should talk about what's happened, don't you?"

What did he mean by that? "You mean about your lucky escape in not having any broken bones?" she joked.

"Sit down here, on the sand for a moment." He removed his jacket, laying it down for them both to sit on. "I mean what happened the day before Christmas Eve when we made love."

"Oh, that's what you call it." Immediately she regretted her harsh words. She looked into his eyes and saw the pain reflected in them. She had wounded him, deeply, that much was obvious.

He picked up a handful of sand and let the grains slowly fall from his hand. "Well, it was to me."

"If it was 'making love' to you, then why did you go off suddenly like that?"

"Because we were disturbed." He kept his gaze lowered.

"No, don't mess with me, Dylan, it was more than that. Look me in the eye."

He brought his eyes to meet with hers and she knew

he was going to tell her the truth. "Okay, if I'm honest with you and myself, it was because I really gave myself to you that afternoon. I was mad at myself for getting carried away and not thinking of contraception. What if I had got you pregnant?"

"I know. It was a bit foolish of us."

"Anyhow, I went to get a bottle of champagne from the cellar to make amends and you had gone."

Would he understand if she explained why she had left that afternoon? She cleared her throat. "Sorry about that, I didn't realise. You see, when you left so abruptly, it felt as if I was being rejected."

"Don't be silly," he said, pulling her to his side. "I could never reject you. I love you too much."

She held her breath, it was the first time he had said those words. It was the first time she had heard them, not just from him, from anyone.

"Oh, Dylan, what are we going to do?"

"What do you mean, what are we going to do? What's stopping us being together?"

"Nothing, I suppose." His mouth hovered inches from hers and their eyes met as he brought his lips crashing down on hers and the waves and the sound of the sea made her feel complete.

****

"Thanks for coming with me today," Dylan said, as they sat drinking coffee back at his quarters. "I think we should begin our Christmas again, don't you?" He waited with baited breath to see how she would respond.

She paused for a moment and gave a soft, gentle smile, one of those smiles that lit up her eyes like two shining stars. "Yes, I think we should. Would you like me have a word with Chef about the preparation? I'm sure if we offer to help out it will put him in a much better mood and encourage him to work a couple of extra hours this evening."

That's what Dylan loved about this woman, she had a way with people. Oh, he knew sometimes in the past she'd had a habit of putting people's backs up, but she had a knack of getting around awkward people. He had been more than impressed with how she had handled his mother in the salon a couple of days back.

"If you like. See if he can cook a turkey for us and tell him we'll pitch in to help with the veg."

"Okey, dokey," she said, jumping up from the sofa. He watched her slip her long stockinged legs into her court shoes and shake back her hair. She smiled again and the corners of her lips appeared to dance with mischief. What a sexy woman she was.

When she had left the room, he limped over to his bureau drawer and looked at the ring again. Dare he ask her tonight? He slammed the drawer shut as she opened the door again unexpectedly. He felt the colour rising to his cheeks.

She didn't appear to notice that he was up to anything. "Oh Dylan, I'll go and check on tonight's guest menu while I'm talking to Chef, anything else you want me to do?"

Had she been a moment earlier she might have seen him return the box to the drawer. "If you can just check that Jim has enough wines and spirits in the bar, that should do for now. Another couple of days, and I should get back to work myself. It'll be quiet for a while until the next wedding party arrives on New Year's Eve. Hopefully, by then, my bruises will have faded. Thanks for your help."

"It's a pleasure." She sent him a look that found its way straight to his heart. He hoped that soon the murderer would be found and they could go back to living a normal life again. Lucy Clarke kept playing on his mind. If they went to see her, would she throw any light on the matter? Maybe she would be too scared to say anything, but with Black out of the picture, maybe she would be more likely to talk.

Stephanie had reminded him earlier to ring Matt and Sandy, but there had been no answer. What on earth could have happened? He felt a bit guilty not being there for his friends. But he had to get himself well again.

He was brought back to reality by a tapping on the door.

"How you feeling today?" Reg entered the room.

"Much better, thanks. Stephanie took me to the hospital for an x-ray earlier. Thankfully, there are no broken bones, but these bruises are looking a lovely colour." He laughed.

"Good to hear it, son." Reg looked as if he was about to give Dylan one of his usual good natured thumps on the arm, but appeared to think better of it. "So how about a whiskey with the old man?"

"I have a half bottle in the cabinet." Dylan rose to his feet.

"No, I meant let's go into the bar for one."

How could he possibly go into the bar? He would have hated it if any of the guests saw him in this state. "I think I'll pass on that one, thanks. It's either here or nowhere."

"Okay. I'll settle for here."

Dylan poured a shot each into two tumblers and they sat facing one another by the fireside.

"So, Dylan...I hear we're having our Christmas dinner this evening?"

"Yes. I thought it would make up for that horrid day we had yesterday."

"Speak for yourself." His father laughed. "I had a great time with your mother. It only turned sour when you and I went to that club."

"So you are both getting on well are you?" This was more than Dylan could have hoped for.

"Well, we were. But I think I've upset her again."

"Oh?"

"I smacked her on the bottom in the corridor in front of those American guests, what's their names now...Howie and Dolly. I think she might have felt humiliated."

"I think you have some major apologising to do, Dad."

"Hmm, maybe I have on a lot of accounts." Dylan wondered what his father meant by that and guessed he was probably referring to the time when he had got her pregnant at such a tender age.

"Look at it this way, Dad, a couple of days ago she wouldn't have given you the time of day. At least you've got her speaking to you now."

They were interrupted by a knock at the door. "I'm just off," Reg said, draining the last of his glass when he saw Stephanie enter. He gave Dylan a wink as he left.

"Ah Steph, I'm glad you've shown up." Dylan got out of his chair. "I was listening to the news on the radio before my father's visit—there's snow on the way. Apparently, there are going to be blizzard conditions for the next couple of days. I think we should try to pay Lucy Clarke a visit now, it may be too late, later on." He picked up a coat and scarf from the stand.

Stephanie frowned. "Do you think you'll be well enough to venture out, Dylan?"

"Don't worry about me, I'll be fine. Go and get your coat and meet me in the foyer in ten minutes."

She nodded.

The sooner they got to Lucy the better, especially for Stephanie's sake.

****

Lucy's flat was at the top of a large tower block in a poor area of Pontcae. The car park was littered with crisp packets, empty cans of lager, and old tyres. Stephanie dreaded to think what else she might find underfoot. She wasn't happy about leaving Dylan's car parked there either.

As they entered the block, the first smell to hit them was a strong odour of urine. No doubt, the foyer was used as a convenient toilet by the drunks and smack heads.

"I'm afraid we're out of luck," Dylan said, pressing the lift button, "it's not working. What floor does she live on?"

"The tenth." She psyched herself up for the long ascent. "Are you sure you wouldn't rather wait in the car?"

"No. I'm not leaving you now."

That's what she loved about Dylan, his caring side. It was obvious that there was no way he was going to abandon her in a rough place like this.

As they climbed the steps, a gang of hooded teenagers pushed past, almost knocking them over. What a place to live. The thing that puzzled her the most was if Lucy Clarke had supposedly stepped into her shoes, then what was she doing in a run down place like this? The money they earned at the club was quite good, surely she could have got a better place to live than this dump?

When they finally got to the tenth floor, Dylan bent over, trying to get his breath back. Stephanie waited a few minutes until she reassured herself he felt strong enough to continue.

"Are you all right?"

"I'm fine." He smiled and laid a hand on her shoulder.

"Good. It's number 103," she said as they dodged their way across the landing in amongst children's toys and lines of washing.

The apartment looked bleak with peeling blue paint on the door and windows. The flat number was painted on the wall in large white, uneven numbers. She knocked on the door, but there was no response. They waited a moment and a thin woman popped her head out of the flat next door.

"Have you seen Lucy Clarke today?" Stephanie asked.

The woman narrowed her eyes. "Ain't seen her for a few days. I keep myself to myself. It's the best way around here." She returned to her flat, slamming the door behind her.

Dylan bent down and peered through Lucy's letter box, then groaned. "I've got bad news…take a look if you have a strong stomach."

Stephanie pulled her hair from her face, slipping it behind her ears, and bent down to take a peek. In the cluttered hallway, slumped, half undressed and tinged blue, was the body of Lucy Clarke. She gasped and turned away, hardly believing her eyes.

"She looks dead to me," Dylan said, his face now grey.

A wave of nausea passed over her. She fought to keep her composure as she felt her legs turn to jelly. Poor Lucy, her involvement with Black had something to do with her death, she was sure of it. The awful realisation hit her that if she had stayed with Black, it could have been her lying there dead in a crummy flat and not Lucy. She shivered. She had to keep control of her senses.

"Give me your phone," Stephanie said, authoritatively, "I'm phoning Dawn Hunter."

****

D.S. Hunter and D.C. Richard Miller arrived at the scene surprisingly quickly.

Hunter peeked through the letter box and said, "We'd better call an ambulance."

"I've already done that," Stephanie said.

"Good. Miller, kick the door down."

The hefty policeman gave the door one sharp kick and it opened easily. Dylan wondered if he should have done that himself, but number one, he was in no fit state to do so, and number two, the girl was obviously dead anyhow. In any case, Miller was built like rugby prop forward. He had the build for it. The couple followed behind the police.

Lucy Clarke had an almost pained expression on her face—it looked as if she had not had an easy death. Her eyes were wide open, staring at the ceiling. They seemed to be taunting the onlookers. Her arms and legs were covered in bruises, some of which looked fresh. Others, by their yellowish appearance, looked old. Dylan wondered what the girl's last thoughts had been—terror filled, probably.

"I feel sick." Stephanie gagged. Dylan put his arm around her. The flat was ice-cold and the smell of death permeated his nostrils.

"Sarge," said Miller, who was looking at something in the corner, "over here..."

Dylan peered over their shoulders and saw a large hypodermic syringe on the floor.

"Don't touch it," commanded Hunter. "We'll wait for the forensic boys."

"What are you two doing here, anyway?" She asked through half closed, suspicious eyes.

"We came to have a word with Lucy," Stephanie explained. Dylan tugged at her arm; he didn't want her to say anything she shouldn't.

"It's okay," she looked at Dylan reassuringly. "I thought Lucy might have been the other woman on the boat the other night."

"I see," D.S. Hunter said sternly. "But you must leave the detective work to us. I was going to pay you a visit later anyhow. You are no longer a suspect in our enquiries."

Stephanie's mouth fell open. "I'm not?"

"No, we know who the murderer is; they left behind a valuable clue."

"Anyone we might know?" asked Dylan.

"I'm afraid I can't say anymore at this point. We may need you to help us with our enquiries further, but you are free to go."

Stephanie appeared to breathe a sigh of relief, but Dylan gritted his teeth. Why had she been subjected to all that interrogation? He shot the policewoman a scathing look and led Stephanie away.

He was relieved to find the car still in one piece when they returned, although there were two young boys eyeing it from across the way.

"The sky's gone very grey," Stephanie said in a whisper. He wished she would say how she felt about all this.

"Yes, it has, let's go home," he said, getting into the car.

By the time they arrived back at the castle, large powdery snowflakes had carpeted the ground and there didn't appear to be any let up.

"Thankfully, we don't have to go anywhere else over the next day or so," Dylan said, preparing himself for a siege situation. They had plenty of food supplies and the wedding guests had booked out that morning. There were only two guests left at the hotel, the American couple: Howie and Dolly, and of course his parents.

****

Stephanie sat on the edge of her bed and contemplated what had happened. It was strange; she had never suspected that Lucy was into drugs. Sure, there were some girls at the club who took recreational drugs, but heroin? That was a completely different ball game. *There, but for the grace of God, go I.*

She was relieved that Dylan had been with her today. If she had found Lucy's body alone, who knows how she would have reacted? And who was the person who had killed Lawrence?

Lifting the receiver by the side of her bed, she attempted to phone Matt and Sandy, but again there was no reply. Perhaps Sandy had already had the baby?

She gazed out of the window.. The snow was still coming down thick and fast. In the distance, she could just about see the lake with its small island in the middle and hoped the swans were all right. She closed the curtains to keep the heat in.

There was something magical about the snow, but on the other hand, there was something about it that made her want to cry. What was it?

Then, it came to her like a flashback in a movie. Daddy had taken her to Switzerland for a holiday before he had left home, just shy of her seventh birthday, and they had had a wonderful time. She remembered the feeling of standing outside. She'd been dressed in a snow suit, wrapped up in a woollen hat, scarf and gloves, trying to catch the snow flakes and letting them land on her nose.

They had gone on the ski-lift to the beginner's slopes and Daddy had gently coaxed her into wearing her skis. She had laughed as she had fallen over again and again and she looked down at the little village below and thought it looked just like the miniature one she had seen in her mother's Christmas catalogue.

In the evenings, they had drank hot chocolate in the biggest mugs she had ever seen, in front of a log fire. They sang her favourite songs and had the greatest time. Daddy didn't explain why Mummy wasn't with them at the time. But later, she had found out that Daddy had been planning to move out and this was his special holiday with her before he left. She was never to see him again. And any chance she ever had of reconciling with him had gone forever when he was killed in a motorcar accident eight months later.

A knock on the door startled her back to reality. Dylan's mother popped her head around the door.

"Can I come in?" she asked tentatively.

"Sure. Come and sit down."

"I hear you had a nasty shock today?" Steph nodded. "But you also had good news?"

"Yes, it seems like the police know who the murderer is, so we can all sleep soundly in our beds."

"I'm not too sure about that." Daphne frowned. "I've just been listening to the news. Whoever it is hasn't been arrested yet."

Stephanie shivered involuntary.

The murderer was still out there somewhere. Was it someone she knew?

Chapter Twelve

Dylan dressed for dinner and laid the table in his quarters with a red table cloth and matching napkins. He'd brought out his best silver service, crystal and glassware for the occasion, topped off with gold candles and a holly centre piece. He stood back and admired his handiwork. Tonight had to be perfect, not only for himself and Stephanie, but for his parents too. It would be the first time they had all eaten together.

He had fond memories of Christmas at his grandmother's small Welsh cottage. Stockings were hung by the fireplace on Christmas Eve and Christmas Day itself was a mixture of church, family and friends. The fun of opening the few small presents she could afford to give to him was the highlight of the day.

This year, he was delighted for her that she had gone away with her friends for Christmas in the Lake District. Doris Evans, a volunteer from the local Cancer Care shop, and Miriam Walker, Matt's mother, were her closest friends.

He gazed out the window. Darkness came early this time of the year. Drawing the heavy drapes, he poured himself another whiskey. Remembering the ring in the drawer he went over and got it out, then slipped it into his jacket pocket for later. This time, nothing could go wrong—he was going to propose to Stephanie, whatever happened. The worst outcome would be that she would turn him down. But that was too awful for him to even contemplate.

****

Stephanie turned off the hob, the vegetables were cooked to perfection. She drained the saucepans in the sink through clouds of steam, and then spooned the potatoes, carrots and brussel sprouts in separate silver tureens and placed lids on top to keep them hot.

For a moment, she felt a shiver run the length of her spine. She had a feeling someone was watching her. She gave a nervous shudder at the thought of her vivid imagination and put it down to the fact the hotel was half empty, giving her a spooky feeling. The blinds were still open, so she quickly pulled them shut.

Daphne came into the kitchen. "Do you want me to take these through?" She asked, referring to the tureens.

"Yes, if you will, I'll bring the turkey and gravy."

She was looking forward to this—it was a far cry from her cardboard dinner at the police station yesterday.

Dylan and Reg were already seated at the table when she arrived, knife and fork in hand. They gave a little cheer of appreciation as she placed the roast turkey in the middle of the table.

Daphne popped the champagne, pouring a bubbling glass of Moet and Chandon for everyone. Dylan held up his glass: "A toast to us all for a Merry Christmas, what's left of it!" Everyone laughed and raised their glasses in appreciation.

During the meal, Stephanie caught Dylan looking across at her occasionally. There was something about his gaze this evening, what was behind it? It was almost as though he could see through to her very soul.

"Crackers!" shouted Reg.

"Pardon?" Daphne laughed.

"I mean you've done a great job with this table," Reg explained, "but you've forgotten to put out the Christmas crackers. You can't have Christmas dinner without the crackers, they're traditional."

Dylan smiled and got out of his seat, returning with four shiny red and green crackers. He gave one each to his parents and handed one to Steph. "Pull a cracker with me, will you?" he asked her.

She blushed as she leaned across the table and jumped a little, startled from the cracking sound. A small, shiny object fell onto the table in front of her.

"It's your prize," she said.

"No, I'm a gentleman, I want you to have it."

She picked it up and placed it in the palm of her

hand, half expecting it to be a cheap metal object, on closer inspection, she could see it was a ring. An expensive looking ring at that.

"It's for you, if you want it," Dylan said, gazing into her eyes.

Daphne and Reg had stopped mid sentence to see what was going on.

"Dylan, it's beautiful." Stephanie examined it closely in her hand. "Is it...?"

"Yes, it is an engagement ring, if you'll have me?" He looked intently at her as if to gauge her reaction.

Reg and Daphne appeared to hold their breath.

This was an unbelievable moment, she had been wrong to have ever doubted Dylan.

"Yes, I'll marry you," she said, wiping away a tear.

Dylan got up and hugged her.

"Congratulations!" shouted Daphne who was on her feet clapping.

Reg followed suit, shaking his son's hand warmly and stretching across the table to plant a kiss on Stephanie's cheek. "Welcome to the family, m'dear!"

"I had no idea." Daphne sniffed into her handkerchief. "I mean, I knew you liked one another, but I didn't realise you were going to get married."

Married. Marriage was something she had managed to avoid up until now. She had been engaged as a young student nurse to a doctor who had let her down badly. Not long afterwards, she had left the profession and taken up with Lawrence Black. It was a time of her life she preferred not to think about. The thought of it still caused her pulse to race. Just because she had been let down all her life didn't mean that Dylan would let her down, did it?

Dylan held her hand as if he could read her thoughts. "It will be okay, I promise," he said as he took the ring and placed it on the wedding finger of her left hand. She smiled up at him through blurry eyes. This was one of the happiest times of her life, so why did she feel so scared and so fragile?

Daphne and Reg looked at one another, taking it as their cue to leave. "Well, we'll leave you young love birds to it," Reg said. "Come on Daphne, let's get a drink in the bar."

****

"You haven't said much," whispered Dylan after his parents had departed. "Is anything the matter?"

"No, Dylan. I am so happy. It's what I really want."

"Then, I suggest we grab another bottle of champagne and take it through to the bedroom." She nodded in agreement and he took her hand in his. As they passed the table, he picked up two glasses and a bottle of champagne.

"I'll just go freshen up." Stephanie watched for a moment as Dylan sat down on the bed and fiddled with the bottle.

"Yes, you do that." He smiled. "And I'll have this opened by the time you return."

He popped the cork and poured the effervescent fluid into two long stemmed glasses. Next, he removed all his clothes except for his red silk boxer shorts and got into the bed. He heard the bathroom door open and Stephanie stood in the doorway. The lights were dimmed, so she was silhouetted there, dressed in a matching bra, panties and stockings.

"Are you ready for me?" she purred. He nodded expectantly as she sashayed over to the bed. Taking his hands, she raised them up onto the pillow behind him. Teasingly, she held them there as he gasped in expectation when she lowered herself on top of him, his erection straining for release from his shorts. Her nipples protruded through the silky material and he longed to touch them.

"I'm going to tantalize you..." she said, licking her lips. Then she brought them down on his. His senses were reeling from her musky perfume and natural feminine odour. He yearned for her to release his hands so he could touch her, but she held them there, firmly. All the time, he felt the sheer softness of her skin on top of his.

She straddled him, keeping a grip on his wrists. He felt her soft mound through her gossamer-like panties, writhing against his hardness. This was agonising pleasure.

"Now, if you're a good boy and get a condom, then the action can begin." She let out a husky laugh.

"No problem," he said through shallow gasps. She

released his hands and he stretched over to his bedside cabinet and produced a pack of three. He handed them to her in eager expectation.

Her laughter ceased as she flipped open the box.

"What's going on?" she asked, the light disappearing from her eyes.

"What do you mean?" He sat up, resting on his elbows.

"There are only two condoms in this box. You must have used one."

"I'm n...n...ot sure," he stammered.

"You couldn't have missed me much when I was in Italy if you were using these. You swore that you and Cassandra had not made love for over a year!"

"We haven't."

"So there must have been someone else," she accused.

"I swear to you, Steph, there has been no one else."

He could tell by her expression that she didn't believe him and who could blame her? He'd hidden the fact that he had a fiancée and now this.

It was a mystery.

He'd had the condoms in his drawer for a long time. If truth were told, he had got them especially for the day of Matt and Sandy's wedding. He and Steph had been getting along so well that he hoped they would get it together. The only thing was, that afternoon they had ended up in a passionate clinch elsewhere in one of the castle bedrooms on the north side of the building, so carried away that any thought of using protection had flown out of the window.

There should still have been three condoms in the packet. Someone must have opened them and taken one, the plastic wrapping had disappeared.

"I'm sorry, I don't believe you," she said, now standing up and grabbing a satin sheet from the bed to cover herself. Now it looked as if she was embarrassed for him to see her body, yet only a moment ago she had appeared totally at ease with her near naked form.

"Steph..." he said, searching for her eyes, but she refused to look at him, choosing instead to gaze in the direction of the window.

"You can have this back!" She removed the

engagement ring and slammed it down on his bedside cabinet. "It seems as though I don't know you at all."

****

Stephanie hurried to the bathroom and banged the door behind her. Hot tears welled up in her eyes and she slid down the door onto the cold tiled floor, huddled like a baby in the womb. Why did life have to be so complicated? Everyone seemed to have baggage from a previous relationship. Everyone dumped on everyone else. People used one another.

Men wanted sex, women wanted love. That was the sum total of it. Dylan hadn't been able to keep it in his trousers when she was away. She could have had her own chances in Italy, but she preferred to return home, back to the man she thought cared about her.

She heard a knock on the door and then Dylan's voice in barely a whisper, "Stephanie, you've got it all wrong you know..."

"Go away!" she shouted through the closed door.

She thought she heard him laugh. "How can I go away? I live here, these are my quarters."

"Go and have a drink in the bar or something while I get dressed. I need some space."

"Uh...okay."

She heard him opening drawers and slamming shut his wardrobe. Then some scuffling about. It sounded as though he was getting dressed. Then she heard him shout something and the door closing behind him.

She got onto her feet and studied her tear stained face in the mirror, cursing herself for being so foolish as to trust another man. Turning on the tap, she washed her face and patted it dry with a towel. Then she got dressed and left the bathroom. As she crossed Dylan's bedroom, she noticed the bed had already been remade. It looked as if she had never been here at all. The engagement ring had disappeared from his cabinet. Maybe that was a figment of her imagination as well.

****

Dylan found his father propping up the bar, his mother nowhere to be seen.

"What's the matter, son? You look like you've dropped a ten pound note and picked up a ten pence piece."

"It's nothing," he lied.

"Don't give me that. Your mother and I left you so you and Stephanie could be together. Now I find you in here with a face like a wet dish rag!"

Dylan looked at the floor and fumbled in his pocket, all the while wondering if he should confide in his father.

He cleared his throat. "Actually, not that it's any of your business, but Stephanie thinks I've cheated on her."

"And have you?"

"Of course not," he snapped.

"All right. Don't bite my head off. Take a drink with me."

Dylan nodded. "Where's Mother?"

"I think she's gone to see how the Christmas pudding is doing. We never got around to having it."

"I see. Well you and her can have it all, I don't want any!" He downed his drink in one go and left the room.

****

Stephanie pulled her suitcase down from the top of the wardrobe. Rummaging through the chest of drawers, she flung her clothes inside the small case, not even bothering to fold them. She had to get out of this place as soon as possible. All her life she had been betrayed, but this was one betrayal too many.

She'd never get a taxi now, the way the snow was coming down thick and fast, unless she walked into Pontcae. Hopefully, tomorrow it would stop snowing and she would be packed ready to leave. Finally, she snapped her suitcase shut, and noticed just one thing remaining of hers—the brooch that Dylan had given her. She picked it up and threw it against the wall. It meant nothing, just like his promises.

Then she lay down on the bed and sobbed. She felt like a prisoner, like she had done yesterday at the police station. This was turning into one, long nightmare, getting worse moment by moment.

If only she had never come back to Wales. If only Dylan hadn't been the one waiting at the airport for her, if only Sandy and Matt had picked her up instead. Taking a deep breath, she realised it was now or never. She picked up her suitcase, marched through the lobby and out through the front door to be met with a familiar face.

"Matt, what on earth are you doing here?" she asked, astonished to see him standing there.

"That's a nice greeting from a friend."

"Sorry, you look like a walking snowman, that's all. It's just that I thought you had to keep an eye on Sandy until she has the baby."

"That's just it. She's gone into labour and I was running her to the hospital as I was told an ambulance might take a long time to get to us with the weather being bad. Unfortunately, we broke down at the bottom of the hill. I can't get a signal on my mobile phone, so I thought I'd try phoning from here."

"Hang on a moment, follow me." She led him into reception and set her case down behind the desk. Use the phone by there," she said.

He had watched her place her case down, but if he thought anything of it, he wasn't saying."

"I can't get a line," he complained.

"Sorry, I should have explained, ring nine first for an outside line."

He did as he was told and finally got an answer. His face looked grim as he set the phone down. "They're not going to be here for at least another hour. What on earth can I do? Sandy's stuck in a car down the lane and she could have the baby at any moment."

"Well, I doubt we'll be able to get one of Dylan's cars out of here with the snow. I tell you what, you go and tell Dylan what's going on and I'll put on a pair of boots and a couple of jumpers and come down to the car with you until the ambulance arrives. Don't worry, I used to be a nurse."

Matt looked at her for a moment and she hoped she sounded more confident than she felt. What other choice did she have? Come to that, what other choice did any of them have?

Dylan was waiting in the lobby when she returned. He looked at her for a second or two, but didn't refer to their last meeting. It was neither the time nor the place. "I thought you might need these for Sandy," he said, handing her a couple of thick blankets, towels and a flask and torch. "Matt's making his way back to the car."

"Thanks," she said, taking them from him. She half

hoped he would say he was coming with her. How could he abandon her, and Matt and Sandy, at a time like this?

****

Stephanie heard Sandy groan as she got near to the car. It had taken her a good ten minutes to get to her, trudging down the lane through thick, icy-cold snow and it kept on coming: huge powdery flakes from up on high.

"It's only me—Steph," she shouted, as she approached with a torch in one hand and a bag containing the blankets, towels and flask in the other. She opened the back door of the car where Sandy was lying awkwardly.

"Oh Steph, thank goodness," Sandy gasped. "Did Matt manage to get through to the hospital?"

"Yes, he did. But unfortunately, they don't think the ambulance is going to get here for over an hour. Are you having any contractions?" Sandy nodded and bit her lip. "Now don't worry, I used to be a nurse, I've helped out with deliveries before."

"Do you think it will come to that?" Sandy asked, wide eyed with panic.

"It might. How often are the contractions coming?"

"About every ten minutes."

Stephanie took the blankets out of the bag and put them over Sandy's perished body. Then she poured the hot tea from the flask and handed it to her to drink. She probably shouldn't give her anything, but the weather was so cold that there was a risk of hypothermia for both Sandy and the baby.

Sandy sipped the hot tea and gave an almighty shriek. Steph flinched for a moment, not knowing what to do or say. Yes, she had assisted at births when she had undertaken a little obstetric training years ago during her general nurse training, but the honest truth was, she had only a small part to play, being more of an observer than anything else. The reality was she might manage to deliver the baby if this was a normal pregnancy, but Sandy's complications petrified her. What if something went wrong? It might mean mother and baby losing their lives. She shivered.

Where on earth was Matt? He should have been here by now.

"I think the baby's coming!" Sandy yelled out.

"Oh, ok...okay." Stephanie said, taking the cup from Sandy and setting it down on a stone wall behind her. "Take nice deep breaths."

Sandy did as she was told. But her breathing sounded rapid and shallow. Steph held her hand. A voice rang out in the distance. "Steph, over here!"

It was Matt. "I can't leave Sandy," Stephanie shouted back.

"Okay. Dylan's coming now, he was trying to get the van out to get Sandy to the hospital." So he hadn't abandoned them at all. How could she have doubted him?

Up the hill, in the distance, two headlights illuminated the swirling snowflakes. He was coming to the rescue.

"It's all right," Steph reassured Sandy. "The Cavalry has arrived."

Sandy frowned. "I don't know if the baby will hang on that long," she said through gasps.

"We'll see." Steph put her arm around Sandy and hugged her. "How often are those contractions coming now?"

"I think about every five minutes." She winced through the pain.

Dylan drew the van alongside the car and got out. "Do you think we have any chance of getting her in the back of the van?" he asked.

"We might do, if we can keep her in a lying position. If we get her to stand upright there's more chance the baby will be born before we are ready." Stephanie hoped she sounded more confident than she felt right now.

Matt finally caught up with them and poked his head through the open car door, giving Sandy's hand a reassuring squeeze.

"I've put an old mattress in the back of the van," Dylan said. "How are we going to get her out of the car? It looks a bit awkward to me."

"I think we have no other option," Matt said. "She'll freeze to death if she stays in there."

Stephanie nodded in agreement. It was time for her to take charge. "Matt, if you take Sandy's top half, and Dylan, you take her legs, I'll support her back. Then if we can carry her to the van and lay her down on the mattress, that will be much better."

"I can't move from here!" Sandy protested when she heard what the trio were planning for her. "I'm in too much pain."

"Look," Steph said, peering in through the car, "it's set to fall to minus ten below freezing tonight. If we stay here, you're putting your baby's life at risk."

"Okay, I'll do whatever it takes, but I'll probably scream my head off."

"Go ahead and scream if it makes you feel better," Steph reassured. "We're all here to support you."

****

Dylan was impressed with Stephanie's handling of the situation. "Are you all right?" he asked, once they had settled Sandy down in the back of the van. She nodded, but didn't say anything. He didn't expect her to. After all, as far as she was concerned he was a philanderer, a cheat. For her to find out about Cassandra was bad enough, they had ridden that wave together, but her last accusation was totally unfounded.

He watched her cover Sandy with the blankets and said, "I'll get her to the hospital as quickly as possible."

Matt held Sandy's hand on one side and Steph comforted her on the other, then Dylan slammed the van's back door and got in the driver seat. He started the engine and drove slowly down the lane. This would be the worse part as it hadn't been cleared. Hopefully, by the time he reached the main road, the traffic would be flowing. It was a shame that Matt hadn't made it to the hospital.

"Drive carefully," Steph ordered, you're bumping about all the over the place.

"Well, excuse me. I'm doing the best I can under the circumstances." What did she expect of him? The ground was like a skating rink.

A loud shriek came from the back of the van and he brought it to a halt. "Sandy's waters have broken—get us to the hospital!" Steph commanded. He did as he was told. If anything happened to mother or baby, he would find it hard to forgive himself. He just had to do the best he could under the circumstances.

When they arrived at the main road, the conditions were much better. It appeared that the gritting lorries had been out, so he was able to put his foot down. They were just ten minutes away from Pontcae General. He hoped they would make it in time.

"What's that noise?" Matt asked from the back.

Dylan glanced in his rear view mirror and saw a blue light heading towards them. It was the police flashing their headlights for him to pull over. Oh no, what a time to do this.

He pulled over to the kerb. "Sorry everyone, it's the police." A collective groan came from the back.

A police officer tapped on the window at the driver's side and Dylan wound it down.

"Do you realise what speed you were going at in these conditions, Sir?" Dylan nodded. "I'd like to see your documents, please."

"Officer, you don't understand..." The policeman eyed him suspiciously. "I have a pregnant woman in the back. She's gone into labour and we're trying to get her to the hospital."

The officer's face broke out into a huge grin. Dylan watched as he walked around to the rear of the van and yanked opened the back door. "Sorry folks," he said, and closed it behind him again. Then he returned to Dylan's side. "Just follow me," he said.

Dylan followed the police car through the town behind the blue light. He hadn't been expecting a police escort, but it was wonderful as several cars pulled over to make way for them.

Dylan heard Steph saying to Matt, "Ring the hospital on my mobile phone to tell them we're on our way."

As they finally stopped in front of the hospital, a porter with a trolley and a couple of nurses were waiting for them to rush Sandy through to the delivery room. Matt accompanied them.

"Thanks, both of you," he shouted as he left. Sandy gave a half wave from the trolley, but she looked to be in too much pain to say much at all.

"Well done," Dylan said to Steph. She smiled and as if remembering the earlier incident, turned her back on him.

"Look, it's freezing out here. Come into the hospital and we'll get a coffee. I don't know about you, but I'm not leaving here until that baby comes into the world."

Hesitantly, she followed him into the building.

****

"Go and get a table and I'll fetch the coffee," Dylan suggested as they entered the brightly lit dining room. It was fairly quiet except for a couple of nurses chatting over their evening meals in one corner and a lone doctor in another.

Stephanie watched Dylan give the waitress his order. She found it hard to believe that it was only a few days ago when he had stood at another counter doing the same thing at the motorway service on the way back from the airport. Then, she had felt apprehensive and a little excited. Now, she didn't know what she felt any more. Lawrence was dead and so was Lucy. Was it the same person who had killed both people? And most importantly of all, why?

She was caught up in such deep contemplation, she hadn't noticed Dylan's arrival. He placed the two cups on the table and looked directly at her. "Sorry, I forgot to ask you if you wanted anything to eat?"

She shook her head. "No, thanks. I think I'm just too wound up about it all."

"You mean what happened with us earlier?"

"Don't flatter yourself," she said, furiously stirring her coffee. Yet, he was right. Of course she was wound up as she had almost found herself having to deliver a baby, but she was also tense due to what had happened. One moment she was having the time of her life on the way to being Mrs Pryce-Jones, the next, the engagement was off with troubling thoughts of another woman being on the horizon.

"Sorry," he said. Then took a sip of his coffee.

"What for?"

"Well, because I wasn't up front with you from the beginning, you have a low opinion of my moral standards."

"I didn't say that."

"As good as."

"Yes, I suppose you are right. After all, what kind of

morals does a man who can't keep it in his trousers have?" She knew she had hit the mark as his face clouded over and his eyes took on a pained expression.

"Steph, I swear to you…" he said, leaning across the table and holding her hand, "I haven't been with anyone else, not since…"

"Since the last time you had me." She finished his sentence for him.

"No, I haven't been with anyone else since that first time at the wedding."

For a moment, her heart strings tugged and she felt herself softening. Maybe he was telling the truth. "Okay," she said finally, "I'm prepared to give you the benefit of the doubt." He let out a long breath. "But, and I stress this is a big 'but', if I find out differently, then all bets are off."

"I can live with that."

"The only thing is, until I'm absolutely sure, I won't be wearing that ring again."

"Okay, fair enough."

She hoped she wouldn't live to regret her decision.

Chapter Thirteen

"Dylan, Steph," a hand tugged at Dylan's arm. Where was he? He realised they had both fallen asleep on the comfy armchairs in the visitors' room.

"What's the matter?" His eyes came into focus and he saw Matt standing in front of him.

"It's time to pass the cigars around!" Matt's face broke out into a broad grin.

"You mean?"

"Yes, Sandy's had the baby!"

"Did you hear that, Steph?" Dylan shook her by the shoulder, trying to rouse her.

Stephanie's eyes flicked open. "Well, what is it?" she asked, looking at Matt.

"A baby girl!" he proudly declared.

Dylan got up on his feet and pumped Matt's hand. "Congratulations, Dad!"

Stephanie smiled. It had all been worth it last night, all that anxiety, all that bother to get to the hospital and she had played a big part in it. "Can we see both mother and baby?"

Matt flopped down on one of the comfy chairs. "In about an hour or so, the midwife said. They want Sandy to rest up for now, I think I'd better have a lie down as well—it's been a long night!"

****

Matt led the couple into a small cubicle offside the main maternity wing. The lights were low, except for a small light above the bed, illuminating both mother and child.

Sandy was gazing adoringly at her newborn baby. She lifted her head and looked at them as they entered the room.

Steph walked tentatively over to the bed, sat down and took Sandy's hand. "I am so pleased for you," she said.

Sandy smiled, her eyes glistening. "I can't believe this beautiful child is ours."

Matt looked at his wife. "You'd better believe it." Then he walked over to the bed and sat down at her side.

Sandy looked at Dylan and Steph. "Thanks for all your help, both of you. We couldn't have done it without you."

Matt gazed at Sandy and the baby and held the infant's tiny hand. "I'll second that."

Dylan came over and stood behind Stephanie and laid his hand gently on her shoulder. Is this what he wanted, too? One day to become a family like this?

"She's absolutely gorgeous," Stephanie crooned. "Do you have a name for her yet?"

Sandy smiled. "We thought, Carys."

"Lovely name," said Stephanie.

****

It was late when they returned to the castle.

"How about a drink?" Dylan suggested.

"Mmm. I'd love one." After the night she'd had, she needed more than one drink. She needed a couple of bottles of wine.

"Go and sit in my lounge and I'll fetch us a couple of special bottles from the cellar."

Stephanie arched an eyebrow. "Vintage champagne," he explained.

"Great. That should go down a treat," she mused.

She sat in Dylan's armchair next to the fire place and kicked off her boots. It was eleven-thirty. She must have dozed off as the next thing she knew she was opening her eyes and the clock showed that it was almost midnight. That was odd. Surely it wouldn't take Dylan half an hour to fetch a couple of bottles from the cellar?

She slipped back into her boots and walked down the corridor in the direction of the cellar. When she got there, the door was slightly ajar.

"Dylan!" she cried out, her voice echoing into the abyss. There was no answer, so she pushed the heavy, creaking door until it opened fully. She searched for a light switch but failed to find one. Perhaps if she walked down the steps, there would be a switch at the bottom.

It was ice-cold as she descended the stone steps that had probably been there for generations. Somewhere down in the very depths of the castle, she heard a faint dripping sound.

Putting both palms on the wall, she scaled her way down in the inky darkness. Good, she found a wooden rail she could hold on to.

Something brushed against her face and she almost cried out with fear. *Just a cobweb*, she reassured herself. *You're losing it, lady.* Maybe this was a daft idea and she should retrace her steps back up to the top. But what if Dylan was lying at the bottom injured? That thought was enough to spur her on.

Finally, she got to the last step and found a switch and the light came on. It was very dim, but at least she had some illumination. She searched around and found a small, dusty table, on top of which was a candle holder and a box of matches. She struck one and lit the candle, just as the light bulb fizzled out.

Shadows flickered in the cellar, casting an eerie impression. "Dylan!" she cried out again. But all was silent. There were rack upon rack of bottles down here. They must be worth a fortune, she mused.

It was no use, she couldn't find Dylan. She was about to go and then let out a gasp, the hairs on her neck standing on end as she saw a woman coming towards her carrying a lighted candle. Then she relaxed, and let out a long breath when she realised it was only her own reflection in an old bar room mirror on the wall.

How silly she was being, imagining all kinds of things. She composed herself and made for the stairs. The cellar door slammed shut and the candle blew out. Terror gripped her as she fought to keep in control of her senses. The thud in her ears deafened her as she heard her own heart beat as loud as a drum. What if no one found her?

"Help!" she tried to shout, but fear made her voice sound weak. "Someone please help me!" Then she put her hands out in front of her to try to find her way out.

Stumbling over something, she tripped and fell, hitting her head against a wine rack. She put her hands out for something solid to help her to get to her feet and touched something soft and warm. It was a human leg, someone was standing by her side.

"Dylan, thank goodness. Help me up."

Two strong hands came towards her and helped her to her feet. Then they forcefully grabbed her from behind, one hand slipping over her mouth. This was her worse nightmare and she had no idea who it was. Trembling, she feared she would black out and then what would happen? Her legs felt like they were going to give way. *I have to do something.* She tried to scream but the large hand was firmly clamped over her mouth.

"Where is it?" the man growled, releasing his hand from her mouth. She inhaled a mixture of expensive cologne and stale cigar smoke. "Don't even think of shouting for help." She was sure she had heard that voice somewhere before.

"I...don't...know what you mean."

"The panda."

What on earth was he referring to? What panda? Did he imagine there was a zoo in the castle grounds or something?

"Don't fuck about. The panda bear for the baby."

"Immediately, the memory came flooding back to the evening she had visited Matt and Sandy. Lawrence had gone out to the car to fetch a huge panda bear as a gift for the new baby. What the hell did this man want with a cuddly toy?

"I don't know what you're talking about," she said, conscious of her trembling voice.

"Don't give me that!" Something sharp and cold stroked her underneath her chin. "This is a knife. Do you want me to use it?"

"N...N...No. Look, the only panda bear I know of is one Lawrence gave as a gift to some friends of ours."

The man relaxed his grip. "These friends of yours...Who are they?" For a moment, she thought she identified the man's voice. His accent wasn't Welsh, this was a London one. Of course, it had to be—Danny King. The trouble was, would she be putting Matt and Sandy in jeopardy if she told him where the bear was?"

"I want that bear!" he demanded with a throaty rasp.

She swallowed. Maybe if she just went over to the cottage and got it for him, he'd leave them all alone. Dylan had their spare key, he used it sometimes to check on the cottage when they were away. It was hanging up, clearly labelled, in his study. Speaking of Dylan—where on earth was he?

"Okay...okay," she relented, "I can get the key and go to their home. There's no one there at the moment. I can get you the bear."

The man let out a long breath. "All right," he said, "I'll just have to trust you." He switched on a torch that he must have had on his person all the while. The light hit his features and she could see that she was right—it was King. He pushed her in front of him.

"Now you know it's me, little Stephanie." He threw back his head and laughed. "My, my, haven't we gone up in the world? What happened to that young hostess who turned tricks down at the club?"

Stephanie swallowed a large lump in her throat. "I never worked as a hostess," she protested, "when Lawrence asked me to do that, I left the club."

"Such a waste," he sneered as he used the blade of the knife to trace the contours of her breasts. For a moment, she feared he would rape her, but this was a man on a mission. When he finally got what he wanted, then he might overpower her. Whatever she did, she had to keep her cool.

"How many people are staying at the castle?" he growled menacingly.

"Myself, Dylan's parents, two Americans, Jim the bartender and the Chef. I make that seven people." Why did he want to know that? "And of course the owner, Dylan Pryce-Jones."

"I've already taken care of him." Stephanie's heart sank. What had King done? Killed him? If anything happened to Dylan, she knew it would be the end of her. She felt her heart swell with love for him. The kind of love she would die for.

"What have you done to him?" she demanded, gritting her teeth.

"Put him out of action for a while, that's all. He's a soft touch, your boyfriend. I know that after he was silly

149

enough to come to the club the other night and ended up with a kicking." Stephanie was seething inside, how she longed to slap King across the face, but that would be a stupid thing to do with a steel blade pressed against her back. "Get up those steps!" he commanded.

She did as she was told, taking each step gingerly, for fear she should fall back onto his knife. What did he have in mind?

When they got to the top, he pushed open the door and closed it again behind them.

"Keep quiet!" he warned.

As they walked along the corridor, he kept the knife at the base of her spine. The hotel was deadly quiet. King starting pushing her down the corridor with his free hand. "One false move and you're dead meat," he whispered harshly.

Stephanie's heart pounded like a hammer drill beneath her jumper. She led King towards the unmanned reception area and in the direction of Dylan's quarters. The sound of a door unlocking startled her. King ducked down behind the reception desk. The door opened and Reg stood before her in his dressing gown. She glanced down at King who gave her a warning look with his eyes.

"Ahh, Stephanie," said Reg, "I hear you've been playing the midwife tonight?"

"Yes, that's right," she said, her voice trembling. Whatever she did, she mustn't endanger Reg. Part of her wanted him to see something was up, but another part of her feared that if he found out, his life could also be in danger.

"A little girl, wasn't it?" Reg persisted. *Please go back to bed.*

"No, it was a boy," Stephanie lied, trying to drop a hint that something was wrong.

"I could have sworn Dylan told me it was a girl." Reg scratched his forehead.

"You've seen him since we came back?" Stephanie was astonished that Reg had seen Dylan.

"Yes, he told me on his way to the cellar."

"He went to fetch a couple of bottles of wine to celebrate Danny's birth."

"Danny?" Reg knitted his eyebrows.

Steph glanced to her left as if to indicate there was someone behind her.

"Yes, Danny. They're going to call him Daniel Lawrence."

The look on Reg's face changed to one of fear. She hoped she hadn't gone too far.

"Well, I'll say goodnight to you, dear," Reg said. Now he was leaving, maybe he hadn't understood the coded message she had tried to send.

"Goodnight, Mr...sorry I've forgotten your name?"

Reg frowned. "It's Mr. Greenaway. Reginald Greenaway."

She held her breath as she hoped King wouldn't cotton on to what she was trying to do—to alert Reg that something was wrong. Watching Reg walk away, she hoped he was sober enough to pick up the coded message, otherwise she was dead meat.

When the coast was clear, King ordered her into Dylan's quarters, where she found the key to Cherry Tree Cottage hanging with other bunches of hotel keys.

"Got the keys to your boyfriend's car?" King ordered. She nodded and slipped them off one of the hooks.

She didn't know which was worse: being subjected to this ordeal by Danny King or being kidnapped by Lawrence Black. At least she had understood a little more of Black's psyche. But Danny King was a different kettle of fish all together. If anything he was more ruthless than Lawrence.

He grabbed the keys out of her hand and marched her in the direction of the main door.

"Which car?" he asked once they were out in the car park.

"Over there," she pointed to the Jaguar. Thank goodness Dylan hadn't parked it in his garage. That really would have complicated matters. Opening the door, he pushed her into the passenger seat. She felt awful about going along with his request, but what other choice did she have?

It took a few minutes for him to scrape the snow off the windscreen and heat up the car to get it started. All the while, she prayed that someone from the castle would realise what was happening to her.

****

Dylan fought to open his eyes, immediately regretting it. His head felt as though it had been trampled over by a dozen horses. Sharp pain pierced his skull. He tried to bring his blurred vision into focus. Staring through the haze, he saw his father. Where were they?

"Are you all right, son," Reg asked, kneeling down on the floor next to him and untying the rope around his wrists and ankles. He removed the gag around his mouth.

"Yes, I'm okay. That King has got one hell of a punch. What about Steph? Has King found her?"

"It looks like it. She tried to give me some sort of message, I think he was watching her every move, that's why I came to find you. It's just as well there are good acoustics in this pantry or I might never have heard you with that gag on. What do you think that fellow wants?"

"I honestly don't know. But he said he wanted me safely out of the way. What are we going to do, Dad?"

"We're going to find them. What about phoning the police?"

"It may take too long."

A sound of an engine being started up vibrated through the window. Although he felt dizzy, Dylan sprang to his feet. "We've got to follow the car," he said, as he watched his Jaguar disappearing down the drive.

****

Stephanie directed King down the lane. They almost got stuck in a snowdrift at the bottom, but she let out a sigh of relief when they finally drew onto the main road.

Due to the atrocious weather conditions, it took a lot longer to get to the cottage than a normal journey would have done. She glanced across at him as he drove.

"What have you done with Dylan?"

"Be a good girl and I'll tell you when I get the bear." He grinned.

She still couldn't fathom what he wanted that bear for. Maybe it was worth something.

They drew up outside the cottage. All was in darkness as she placed the key in the lock.

"Be as quick as you can!" he commanded. "I don't want to get caught here." Caught for what? Kidnapping a panda bear?

Stephanie trembled as she searched through Matt and Sandy's personal possessions, perspiration forming on her brow. This was wrong. But what other choice did she have if she didn't want them wrapped up in all of this? It was better to find the bear and get King out of here. Once he had what he wanted, he wasn't likely to stick around.

The first logical place to search was the baby's bedroom. It broke her heart to rummage around in the newly decorated nursery with its new white bassinette and matching furniture.

There were several fluffy toys scattered around, but none of them was a panda bear. What if she failed to find it? What then?

She searched through Matt and Sandy's bedroom but found nothing there either.

Going downstairs, she looked in the wall unit and in the kitchen cupboards. She was just about to sink into the depths of despair when she opened the cupboard under the stairs. The large panda bear tumbled out, hitting her in the face.

"Found it!" she shouted at King. He rushed down the stairs, two at a time, and grabbed the bear from her grasp.

Then she watched in astonishment, as he ripped off its head and delved inside the wadding, producing a small brown paper package.

"Drugs?" she asked. King shook his head.

"Diamonds," he gloated and his face broke into a huge grin of triumph. "Good girl. That bastard Black was supposed to hand this over to me after his little Amsterdam trip last month." He kissed the package.

"What now?" she asked.

"These little beauties are going to make me a fortune!"

****

"What's going on with you and Stephanie?" Reg asked as Dylan tried to concentrate on the road. What a time for an interrogation.

"What do you mean?"

"Well, things seem to have cooled off since the announcement of your engagement yesterday."

"She thinks I've let her down. It's all a

misunderstanding, really."

"Misunderstanding?" It was obvious to Dylan that his father wasn't about to give up. Once started, he was like a dog with a bone. This was going to be embarrassing, but the only way to shut him up was to tell him the truth.

"After we all had dinner, Stephanie and I retired to the bedroom. Well, you can guess what for."

"I understand."

"But when things got a little heated, we were about to use a condom from what I thought was a new pack of three, but one was missing. Of course, being a woman, she put two and two together and came up with six."

"You mean, she thought you had slept with someone else?"

"Something like that." Dylan's face was growing hot with embarrassment.

For a long while, his father remained silent. "I'm sorry, son," he said, "it was my fault."

"How on earth could it be your fault, Dad?"

"Err...I took one from the packet, in case I needed it." Did he want to hear this?

"You mean for you and Mum?"

"Your mother. Yes. We'd been getting on so well that I hoped something might happen between us. Although after what happened all those years ago, I wanted her to know that I was going to act responsibly this time."

Never in a million years had Dylan guessed what had happened. It was hard to think of two people of their ages getting it on. His mother was a lot younger than his father, she would be fifty next year, so technically, it could still be possible for her to get pregnant.

His father carried on, "I think there will be little chance of that happening now. She told me this morning that Donald is invited here for the New Year."

He could hear the desolation in his father's voice. This isn't what he wanted, he wanted his parents to be reconciled. He had hoped that his mother would have forgotten all about Donald by now.

"Never mind, old fellow," Dylan tried to cheer him up, "there's still a couple of days left to win her over, before he turns up."

****

"Well, you've got what you came for, so I'll be off," announced Stephanie.

She didn't like the way King was looking her up and down. She made to go out through the front door and he seized her by the wrist and spun her around until she was face to face with him. Very close.

"Not so fast," he said. "I've always fancied you, but you thought you were a cut above the other girls. You teased me when you wore those low cut blouses and short skirts at the club."

"B...but they were just an outfit I was expected to wear. It was all a show," she protested.

He pulled her even closer and pressed his lips violently down on hers. She struggled, but he was strong. He pushed her backwards so that she was pinned up against the wall.

"Little Miss Tease," he taunted. With one hand he lifted her jumper and found her breast and gave it a squeeze and then let out a groan.

Bile rose to her throat and her stomach heaved as she felt his erection against her leg. She trembled as she knew what he was about to do. He was going to rape her, she was sure of that. Maybe her only chance was to go along with what he wanted for time being, at least there was less chance of getting hurt that way.

"Come on, Steph. You want this, girls like you say 'no', when they mean 'yes'."

Her breaths came fast and shallow. She nodded and he started to undo his belt.

"Look behind you!" she shouted. As he turned his head, she kicked him between his legs and left him doubled up on the floor.

"You fucking bitch!" he shouted, as he tried to get on his feet.

She ran for the door and fiddled with the lock, her fingers slipping with perspiration. Finally, she managed to open it and ran down the drive as fast as she could, but slipped on the icy pavement.

A hand descended on her and pulled her up by the hood of her jacket. What was he going to do now? He brought his hands to her throat and shook her violently. *He's going to strangle me.* Everything became blurred as she fought to remain conscious. She desperately tried to prise his hands away from her throat but her strength was slowly zapping away as the pressure on her throat increased and a gurgle escaped from her lips.

In the distance, a car door slammed, and voices came towards her, but she didn't know if she was hallucinating or if they were real. The grip was like a vice, he didn't want to let go. *Help me, someone, please.*

She was falling, falling, as his grip loosened, she hit the pavement with force.

****

"You bastard!" Dylan shouted as Stephanie hit the ground. Reg rushed over to her as Dylan grappled with King.

"Watch out, he's got a knife!" Reg shouted.

Dylan side stepped as King lunged towards him.

"Nice little girlfriend you have," King sneered. "I could have had her if I'd wanted. She was really up for it."

Dylan's breath came in short bursts. *I'm going to kill the sonofabitch! How dare he hurt the woman I love.* Dylan gave a loud cry and ran at King, head butting him in the stomach, momentarily winding him. As the man staggered backwards, Dylan grabbed the hand that held the knife. King was strong for sure, but he hadn't banked on the strength Dylan had after what the brute had done to Stephanie. King lost his grip and the knife clattered on to the pavement.

Dylan lunged at King and dragged him up by his lapels. The man tried to catch his breath but Dylan got behind him and brought his elbow in front of the man's throat, putting him in a head lock. He heard a siren in the distance moments before a blue light pulled up in front of them.

Hunter and two other police officers rushed out of the car, grabbing hold of King.

"Daniel Joseph King you are being arrested for the murders of Lawrence Black and Lucy Clarke. You do not have to say anything, but it may harm your defence if you do not mention when questioned something which you later rely on in court. Anything you do say may be given in evidence…"

King let out a long groan as one of the officers cuffed

him.

"Put him in the car," Hunter commanded.

"Nice work," she said to Dylan, patting him on the shoulder. "Is Stephanie all right?"

"I'm okay," Stephanie sat up on the pavement, massaging her sore neck.

"Maybe you'd better get a check up at the hospital?" Advised D.S. Hunter.

"I think I've had enough of hospitals for one day." Steph smiled ruefully. Dylan rushed over to her side and helped her onto her feet.

"He's got a package on him," Stephanie explained, "he was after a cuddly toy that Lawrence Black had given to Matt and Sandy's new baby. It was stuffed with diamonds."

"Yes, we know all about that," the policewoman said. "You see, when we examined Lawrence's boat, we knew that someone had been looking for something illegal, we assumed it was drugs. The furnishings had been ripped apart. That's why Black was probably killed."

"We got a call from Lucy Clarke, telling us about the diamonds in the panda bear. We knew it would only be a matter of time until we flushed the murderer out. Unfortunately, Lucy Clarke was given a bad batch of heroin by King. He wanted to shut her up, but he was too late. She was the other female on the boat the night Black died, we think she'd gone to warn him that King was after those diamonds, and of course, she must have been the one who opened the door to the boat, as she had a spare key."

Stephanie's stomach lurched as she realised it was probably Lucy who had painted that lipstick message on her mirror. The girl had wanted to scare her away from Black. She was probably in love with him. What a high price to pay. "So King's responsible for two deaths?" asked Dylan.

"Yes." Hunter made her way to the car.

"But what about the missing girl Jenni? Didn't he kill her?" Stephanie asked.

She smiled. "No, she's alive and well. She's the one who helped us out on this case, we were keeping her in a safe house while investigations were ongoing."

"But I heard King boasting that he had killed her," Dylan said.

"That maybe so," Hunter explained, "but he wasn't telling the truth. That's what he wanted his men to think."

"Well, we'd better get you home," Dylan said, wrapping his jacket around Stephanie's shoulders.

"One more thing," shouted Hunter, "I'll need you both to give a statement about what happened tonight. Get some shut eye and I'll see you at the station in a few hours."

Stephanie let out a sigh.

"Don't worry," Dylan comforted her, "it's not going to be anything like the last time you were at the police station."

****

Reg drove them back to the castle and Stephanie snuggled into Dylan in the back seat. Dylan had said he was taking her home and home is where she belonged, safe in the arms of the man she loved.

Chapter Fourteen

Dylan followed Stephanie into the castle as far as her bedroom door. Lowering his head, he kissed her goodnight.

"Are you okay, now?"

"I'm fine. Honestly, I am. Just got a little sore throat that's all," she joked. "I thought my end had come when King had my neck in a vice-like grip, but when I saw you arriving, I knew everything would work out fine."

"If he had done anything to you..." Dylan said, stroking her neck. "Well, I'd better let you get your beauty sleep."

"Do you have to go?" She cast her gaze toward the floor as she forced the words out.

"Err," He cleared his throat. "I suppose I could come in for a bit."

She unlocked the door and removed her jacket, scarf and boots. "Pour me a glass of sherry to warm me up, would you?"

He removed his jacket, went over to the mini bar and got a small bottle of sherry out and poured it into two schooners.

"That's better," she said, licking her lips and placing her empty glass down on the cabinet. "I think I'd like to take a shower, how about you?"

"Steph..." Dylan began, "there's something I need to tell you...come and sit on the bed next to me."

She walked over and sat down. "What is it?" Her chocolate brown eyes searched his.

"It's about the missing condom business."

"Oh that," she replied nonchalantly.

"Yes, that. I found out what happened."

"Listen, Dylan. I trust you enough to realise you were

telling me the truth."

"No, please, let me explain. I found out it was my father who had removed one from the packet. He told me to tell you. He was too embarrassed to do so himself."

"Your father?" she asked incredulously.

"Seems the silly old dog thought he was going to get lucky with my mother." Dylan let out a little laugh.

Stephanie smiled. "Well, now there's no barrier between us." She took his hand and led him towards the bathroom.

"What about protection?" he asked.

"Don't worry. I've thought of that." She delved into her handbag and produced a packet of three. "I got a pack out of the ladies' room in the foyer earlier. It's a good job you cater for all the needs of your guests." She laughed.

He had to admit, she'd thought of everything. He scooped her up in his arms and carried her to the shower room, then set her down and hungrily brought his lips down onto hers. She softened in his embrace.

Touching her, feeling her warmth in his arms, he melted.

Deftly, she unbuttoned his flannel shirt and tossed it on the floor. She rained kisses on his chest, then downwards towards his stomach, where he let out a low moan. He stiffened beneath his trousers. She went down on her knees and loosened his leather belt. His hands moved to her head, into the silky softness of her hair, as she unbuttoned his jeans.

Stepping out of his denims, he brought her back to her feet. He lifted up her jumper and pulled it over her head, revealing the most perfectly formed breasts. They seemed to yearn for release from her bra. He embraced her, unclipping it with one hand.

"My beautiful, Steph," he murmured, his hands moving towards her breasts.

"Not just yet," she teased.

He brought his hands to her slacks and helped her undo them. She was left in just a silky pair of panties. She reached down and turned the shower on.

"Here let me," he said, untying the ties on the side of her panties.

He followed her into the cubicle and they stood

underneath the shower head, liberally sprayed by the pulsating, hot water.

She passed him the shampoo and he washed her tresses. The soft, herbal essence, sent his senses into overdrive. Then, she returned the favour, gently massaging his scalp. *This feels so good, having her so close to me.* They rinsed off under the power shower, Stephanie letting out a little giggle every now and then. *It's great to see her so happy.*

She let out a moan as he picked up the bar of soap and rubbed it on a sponge, then started to sponge and massage her breasts. They were the most beautiful breasts he had ever seen. He lowered his head to take one of the firm nipples in his mouth and she gasped. She held his head there as if keeping him where he was. He flicked his tongue over her nipples in light, feather like motions.

He brought his lips to hers again and she tilted her head back so the water drenched her face. His hands moved behind her and roamed over her back, towards her buttocks. He brought her close to him and squeezed.

****

His erection stood firm against her pulsating mound. She had to have him inside her now. He teased her a little by moving away, creating a distance between them. She took the soap from the shelf and lathered up her hands. His nearness both frightened and excited her. She ran her fingertips over his well honed chest. His breastbone was covered with a smattering of hair and she ran her hands through it, hoping to bring him to fever pitch.

Lathering up both hands again, she gently massaged him so that he remained proud and erect while she tantalised him with her touch. He let out a low groan of pure ecstasy as she continued to run both hands up and down his length, both pleasing and teasing him. Then, she moved from under the spray, letting the water rinse him clean.

Unexpectedly, he grabbed her and pushed her up against the wall of the shower cubicle. The contrast of the cold, wet tiles against the hot steamy shower was both sensual and stimulating. She felt him again, there, near her special place. Breathing heavily, she quivered and gave herself up wantonly—writhing with lust. Parting her with his fingers, he slowly entered. She let out a gasp and he was inside of her, filling her, feeling so damn good.

Rhythmically, he pumped and she moved with him as if they were one being. His grey-green eyes compelled her to gaze into them. Lost in the sea of his soul, moving like a wave on the ocean, she responded. She licked his index finger and he let out a groan. How she wanted to please this man, but she also knew he equally wanted to please her too. She realised for the first time that he would never abandon or reject her.

She cried out with joy as a quiver ran from her inner thighs and over her abdomen...finally giving her release. Moments later, she felt him tense as a moan of ecstasy passed his lips. For the first time in her life, she discovered what it was like to give herself, body and soul, to someone.

For a long time, they stood embracing under the hot shower, unable to speak, their breaths coming in shallow gasps. Finally, Dylan brought his hand to her face and turned it towards his.

"I love you so much, Steph. It almost hurts," he revealed.

She nodded. She felt the same way about him. It was as if they were two halves of the same whole, now fitting together perfectly.

"I think we'd better dry ourselves." She turned off the shower and handed him a towel. She expected him to dry himself, but instead he used it to towel her hair and body, slowly and sensually. Then he handed her one of the cotton robes hanging behind the door that were kept for guests. He quickly towelled himself down and also put on a robe. Then he swept her up in his arms and carried her through to the bedroom.

It had been one hell of a night and now at last they could fall asleep, safely, in one another's arms.

Epilogue

Reg adjusted his tie, checking his wristwatch for the umpteenth time that evening as they dined on New Year's Eve, all together in Dylan's quarters.

"What's the matter, Dad?" Dylan spoke softly, putting his hand on his father's shoulder in quiet reassurance.

"I'm just a bit apprehensive about what will happen when Donald arrives."

"Don't worry," Dylan grinned. "Mother has something to tell you. Don't you, Mother?"

Daphne leaned across the table. "Donald won't be coming, Reg."

"Why ever not?" Reg asked in bewilderment.

"Because in the end, I decided I just didn't want him here. I'd rather be with you." She stretched out her hand and gave Reginald's a squeeze. For once, he was speechless. Dylan thought he could see a tear in his eye. Mimi gave a little yap, as if she was in total agreement with her mistress's decision.

"Steph, come with me a moment, will you?" Dylan took her by the hand. Stephanie wrinkled her brow in puzzlement. It would be midnight in a couple of moments, time to see the New Year in. "And you two, as well," he said, addressing his parents. "Although I would suggest you leave Mimi locked in here for a while." Daphne raised her eyebrows in surprise.

Dylan held Stephanie's hand tightly as they ran down the corridor, giggling like two teenagers. He walked her through the unlit ballroom, the sounds of their footsteps echoing until they stood at the French doors. Thrusting them open wide, he led her outside onto the terrace.

In the distance, she heard the church clock begin to strike twelve.

"Look!" he said, pointing to the sky.

She gazed up at the velvet, inky darkness, wondering what he was referring to, and then heard an almighty bang as a shower of fireworks exploded, lighting up the night sky with a myriad of colours.

Against the wall, outside in the garden, colourful lights illuminated to spell out the words: 'WILL YOU MARRY ME?'

"Oh yes, Dylan. I'll marry you," she said, and he brought his lips onto hers for a kiss that seemed to go on forever, as if neither wanted it to end...

When at last he lifted his head, he held her at arms' length and said: "I'm so glad you said that. Otherwise I wouldn't have been able to return this to you."

He slipped the engagement ring back on her finger where it belonged.

Dylan's parents arrived in time to see the ring returned to its rightful place, all four of them hugging as a profusion of fireworks continued to go off in the castle grounds around them.

It was as if the celebration was to welcome her back to her home and her man. She smiled...knowing she was beginning a new year of a new life.